Readers have fallen for Gianna Z.

An E. B. White Read Aloud Award Winner

"Laced with humor and heart. . . . An insightful and affecting read." —*Booklist*

"Messner's warm and humorous tone will capture even reluctant readers." —*SLJ*

"An engaging saga." —*Kirkus Reviews*

"Messner not only reached the finish line with *The Brilliant Fall of Gianna Z.*, she won the gold and the crowd went wild." —TeensReadToo.com

BOOKS BY KATE MESSNER

The Brilliant Fall of Gianna Z.
Sugar and Ice

The Brilliant Fall of Gianna Z.

Kate Messner

Walker & Company

For my parents, Tom and Gail Schirmer,
who brought me up with books to read, trails to explore,
courage to dream, and love to back it all up. Thanks.

And for all the Global Citizens
who have gone out collecting leaves . . .

That which does not kill me makes me stronger.
—Friedrich Nietzsche

First published in the United States of America in September 2009 by
Walker Publishing Company, Inc., a division of Bloomsbury Publishing, Inc.
Paperback edition published in September 2010
www.bloomsburykids.com

For information about permission to reproduce selections from this book, write to
Permissions, Walker BFYR, 175 Fifth Avenue, New York, New York 10010

The Library of Congress has cataloged the hardcover edition as follows:
Messner, Kate.
The brilliant fall of Gianna Z. / by Kate Messner.
p.   cm.
Summary: Gianna has less than one week to complete her leaf project if she wants to compete
in the upcoming cross-country sectionals, but issues like procrastination, disorganization—and
her grandmother's declining health—seem destined to keep her from finishing.
ISBN-13: 978-0-8027-9842-8 • ISBN-10: 0-8027-9842-X (hardcover)
[1. Grandmothers—Fiction. 2. Old age—Fiction. 3. Friendship—Fiction.
4. Trees—Fiction. 5. Running—Fiction. 6. Schools—Fiction.
7. Family life—Vermont—Fiction. 8. Vermont—Fiction.] I. Title.
PZ7.M5615Br 2009   [Fic]—dc22   2008046979

ISBN 978-0-8027-2173-0 (paperback)

Book design by Nicole Gastonguay
Typeset by Westchester Book Composition
Printed in the U.S.A. by Quad/Graphics Fairfield, Pennsylvania
2 4 6 8 10 9 7 5 3

All papers used by Bloomsbury Publishing, Inc., are natural, recyclable products
made from wood grown in well-managed forests. The manufacturing processes
conform to the environmental regulations of the country of origin.

Earth's the right place for love:
I don't know where it's likely to go better.
I'd like to go by climbing a birch tree
And climb black branches up a snow-white trunk
Toward heaven, till the tree could bear no more,
But dipped its top and set me down again.
That would be good both going and coming back.
One could do worse than be a swinger of birches.

—from "Birches" by Robert Frost

CHAPTER 1

Forty-one minutes to cross-country practice.

Forty-one minutes to shorts and running shoes.

Forty-one minutes to crisp October air that smells like apples and leaves and wood smoke all at once.

And that means forty-one more minutes of science class.

I try to catch Zig's eye, but he's busy taking notes, so I look around while Mrs. Loring lectures us about the wonder of trees. Her dark eyes are huge behind her glasses, like she has the most exciting news ever.

"Did you know there are probably more than twenty *thousand* species of trees in the world?"

I don't think Kevin Richards knew, and I'm pretty sure he doesn't care. He's wadding up tiny balls of paper, trying to shoot them into the desk in front of him. Ruby Kinsella's sitting there, but she's too busy writing in the green marble notebook she always carries around to notice she's under attack. I hear a rustle behind me and turn to see Bianca Rinaldi rummaging through her backpack for lip gloss.

"Twenty thousand!" Mrs. Loring says. "And scientists think there may be a thousand different species in the United States alone."

That's a lot of trees. I pull out my sketchbook and start doodling some of them. I wish I had my colored pencils.

The clock ticks.

Forty minutes.

Forty minutes of Bianca kicking my desk and smirking about the fact that Dad drove me to school in the hearse this morning. I argued, but it didn't do any good.

"It has four wheels and runs fine. It'll get you there," he said.

"Four wheels and a huge sign that says 'Zales Funeral Home' on the side," I said. "I might as well show up at school with a coffin strapped to the roof." But he had a pickup at nine, and Mom needed the van anyway.

It's been Bianca's favorite topic of conversation all day.

"Poor Gianna. *Imagine* having to ride around in a car full of dead bodies," she whispers to Mary Beth Rotwiller, and they crack up. I look down at my sketchbook where I've penciled in the classroom window, the trees outside, the track I wish I were running on right now.

Thirty-nine minutes.

"So," Mrs. Loring says, "given all those different kinds of trees, completing your leaf collection should be a piece of cake. I'd like to review the requirements one last time. Please take out the project packet I gave you."

I pull my science binder from my backpack and flip through the papers, but I can't find the leaf project stuff. It might be in my locker. Here's a French handout on parts of the body I'm supposed to be studying for a quiz next week.

"Psst. Gianna!" Zig slides his desk a little closer to mine. "Look on with me," he whispers.

Zig is my lost-homework hero. Mom says I have attention issues. Zig has the opposite of attention issues. I bet he could find his second-grade name tag if you asked him. And it wouldn't even be wrinkled.

"Here." He points to the list of requirements on his paper as Mrs. Loring reads them off.

"You need twenty-five different leaves. You'll organize and catalog them, label each leaf with its common and scientific names, its geographical range of distribution, its primary characteristics, and its main uses. You should find a creative way to display your leaves. And I expect you to meet all your deadlines. The final project is due one week from today."

"One week. Got that?" Zig whispers and nudges me with his elbow. I nudge him back. Okay, it's more like a sharp poke, actually. But he knows better than to tease me about deadlines. My brain and deadlines have never gotten along, but finish lines are a whole other story. I'm only good with time if it has to do with running.

Which reminds me. Thirty-four minutes.

"Your first deadline is rapidly approaching," Mrs. Loring says, tapping the big "OCTOBER 11TH" she's written on the blackboard. "I want to see ten leaves by Monday to make sure you're on track."

I *wish* I were on the track. I look out the window. Thirty-two minutes.

"Then you'll need to have all twenty-five leaves collected and identified by next Thursday so you'll be ready to turn in the final project on Friday," Mrs. Loring says, and smiles out over our desks. She's sure we're all well on our way.

Not.

She reviews how to use a leaf identification key, even though she's sure we've mastered that by now.

Not.

She reminds us that she has poster board and binders available if we need them, but she's sure we've all taken care of materials by now.

Not.

She reminds us how much fun this project is going to be. Double not.

I open my sketchbook again and scratch in a big barren tree with branches as empty as my leaf collection is right now. I'll start collecting tomorrow. How hard can it be?

I draw in the sports field with soccer nets standing guard at each end. We'll be out there for cross-country today, too, doing our track workout. I sketch the oval that rings the field and try to texture it with the edge of my pencil to make it look gravelly.

Finally, the bell rings, so I don't have to settle for just drawing the track. I sign my sketch at the bottom—

Gianna Z.

—because artists should always sign their creations. I grab my notebooks and head for the door.

"Two weeks to sectionals. Two weeks!" Coach Napper tweets her whistle to mark the end of our last 800-meter run. It echoes high and sharp against the brick wall in back of the school. "You need to get a move on, Zales!"

"Huh?" I stand up from my lunge stretch. What's she talking about? I just had my best run of the week. "I'm set, Coach. My times have been—"

"Your *times* are fine. I'm talking about your science grade. Coach Loring—*Mrs.* Loring—just came over from the soccer field to talk with me. No passing grade—no sectionals. I'll have to send your alternate." Coach nods at Bianca Rinaldi, who's just jogged up to us.

"Oh, wouldn't that be *sad*?" Bianca turns her lip-glossy mouth into a phony pink frown. "But I'm ready if you need me, Coach. *I've* knocked ten seconds off my regular four-mile time in the past two weeks." She tugs at the bottom of her purple stretchy T-shirt so it almost covers her belly. The silver sparkle letters on it spell out, *It's not how you play the game; it's how you look when you play the game.*

"Keep working on it, Bianca." Coach nods. Bianca tosses her ponytail and trots over to Mary Beth Rotwiller, sitting on the steps.

This is *not* happening. Bianca Rinaldi isn't a runner. She might look like a model for running shorts, but she's not a runner. She's not breathing hard. She's not sweating. There's no mud on her sneakers, not even on the bottoms. You can't run cross-country with clean sneakers.

Coach can't send Bianca.

I say it out loud. "You *can't* send her."

"I have to send her if you're not eligible. Take care of it." Another tweet of the whistle, and everyone heads for the locker room.

I pull open the door and a blast of hot, wet air hits me— a haze of shower steam, sweat, and body splash. I go to the sink, splash cold water on my face, and look up to wipe the drips off my pointy chin. If it's really how you look when you play the game that counts, I've got trouble. My curly red hair frizzes itself into a bad imitation of a shag carpet when I sweat. My cheeks turn the color of ripe strawberries anytime I run, so even if I'm not really pushing it, I look like I'm about to pass out.

"You okay?" Ellen Frankenhoff's face appears in the mirror over my shoulder. "You're kinda red *à la visage*."

"Huh?"

She pats her cheeks. "*Visage* means face. We need to know it for the quiz." Ellen is in my French class and has clearly been studying more than I have. I hope I remembered to put those notes in my backpack.

"My face is always kinda red." I turn and reach for my wind pants on the bench behind her.

"Tell me about it. Exercise is so overrated." Ellen pulls on her sweatshirt. Her glasses get stuck in the hood, so I reach over to help her get untangled.

"You're getting faster, though," I say. "You're doing really well for a new runner." Ellen never meant to be a new runner. She was perfectly happy going to Recycling Club after school, but her mom signed her up for the cross-country team after she saw a new report on adolescent obesity.

"Oh, Ellen's gotten *lots* faster, hasn't she?" Bianca tosses her empty water bottle on the floor, steps up to the mirror to smooth her already-smooth blond hair, and smirks. "Maybe *she'll* be your alternate when you fail science, Gianna."

"Gianna's not going to fail science," Ellen says to Bianca's reflection, just as Coach steps into the locker room behind us.

"Well, good." Bianca whirls around so fast I have to jump to avoid getting swatted with her ponytail. She glances at Coach and grins. "I'm sure you have everything under control, Gianna. You probably have that leaf collection half done by now, *right*?"

My running shirt feels like it's tightening around my chest, and as Bianca bounces off to meet Mary Beth, I sink down on the bench next to Ellen. "She knows. How does she know? How could she know I'm behind on that project?"

Ellen doesn't say anything.

I look up at her. "Because I'm late with everything?"

She smiles, but not in a mean way. "Bianca and Mary Beth are like bloodhounds. They sniff out your weaknesses."

That makes me laugh a little.

Ellen tilts her head. "What's so funny?"

"Nothing, really. It's just that Zig and I play this game where we figure out what dogs people would be if they were dogs. We always had Bianca and Mary Beth pegged as pit bulls."

Ellen smiles, too. "Maybe they're mutts—like a pit bull–bloodhound mix."

"Always ready to go in for the kill."

Ellen sighs. " 'Fraid so, Gianna. Bianca's dying to go to sectionals. She'll do anything to make sure there's a reason they need her as an alternate."

"Terrific." I take a deep breath. "You need a ride home?"

Ellen nods. "If it's okay."

"Fine with me—if you don't mind riding in the hearse."

"Empty, right?"

"It's always empty when Dad picks me up. He says it's

disrespectful to expect the dead to go along schlepping kids all over the place. They've done their time."

"Yeah, I'd love a ride. And Bianca's probably gone by now so we won't have to listen to the corpse-car jokes." She picks up Bianca's water bottle from the locker room floor and tosses it into the recycling bin with a sigh. "Did you know Americans throw away thirty million of these things every day?"

"Wow." That's a lot of water bottles. There must be something someone could make out of those.

I grab my duffel bag in one hand and my backpack in the other. "Coach *can't* replace me at sectionals. She can't. Bianca has glitter letters on her shirt. That's just not right."

Ellen and I step outside, and Dad's there waiting in the long black car with Zales Funeral Home printed in big silver letters on the side. All the windows are down, and he's playing the Beach Boys full blast. Thank God everyone else is gone.

By the time we drop Ellen off at her house and swing by to pick up the spinach Mom wants from the farm market, it's after five.

Zig's waiting for me on the porch steps next to our Halloween pumpkins, attaching a motorized propeller to the back of some LEGO thing.

I slam the hearse door and walk over. "Hey!"

Zig holds up one finger but doesn't look up. He can't talk and think at the same time, so I plop down next to him to wait. The bricks are warm from the late afternoon sun, even though the air's cooling down by the minute. I run my hand over the biggest of the five pumpkins we picked from the field at the Parkinson farm last weekend. We won't carve them until the night before Halloween, but we always put them out early to brighten up the porch. My little brother Ian's pumpkin is the huge one; he's only six, so Dad had to carry it for him. Dad's is short and sort of squatty, like him. Mom's is perfectly round, without a single scratch or mark on it. Nonna's is tall and skinny and a little bit crooked. And mine is medium-sized with a big knobby bump toward the bottom that looks like a witch's chin.

I'm figuring out where the eyes will go when Zig finally looks up. "Hey."

"What's that?" I nod at his twirly LEGO thing.

"A battery-operated, multi-environment hovercraft."

"Which is . . . ?"

"A motorized, air-propelled vehicle that can operate on land, water, or, most importantly, ice. The Coast Guard uses them on the lake when ice fishermen get stuck out there."

"Does the Coast Guard make theirs out of LEGOs, too?"

He puts down his LEGO-mobile and gives me a shove. "Too bad you're being such a dork. I came over to see if you wanted help with your leaf project."

"In that case, please accept my humble apologies. I'm sure your hover-ma-callit will kick the Coast Guard's butt."

He grins, brushes a flop of black hair from his eyes, and reaches for his school stuff. "I collected a few extra leaves you can have." He presses a keypad to disarm the buzzer alarm he rigged up on his backpack zipper to keep Kevin Richards from stealing his math homework. "Here you go."

He hands me a clear plastic bag with leaves inside. It's

labeled with blue marker; one leaf is a linden, and one's a tulip maple.

"Thanks."

"How many do you have so far?" he asks.

I pick up a couple of long pine needles from the step and poke them against one another. "Hey! This is kind of like sword fighting, huh?" I get a long one in each hand so they can do battle.

"Gee . . . have you even started?"

My right hand picks up a little leaf to use as a shield and is about to win the whole fight, but Zig snatches it away.

"I have a few," I say.

"How many?" He stares me down.

"Okay, fine. Two." I hold up his linden and tulip maple leaves.

Not many people can get to me like Zig. His real name is Kirby Zigonski Junior, but he's always been Zig to me. We've been friends since third grade, when he sat behind me in Mrs. Light's class, right next to Lawrence, our classroom iguana. With names like Zigonski and Zales, we've been homeroom and locker neighbors ever since.

"Want me to help you find more tomorrow?"

I nod as Mom sticks her head out the door. "Dinner!"

"Hey, Mom! Okay if I go out collecting leaves with Zig in the morning?"

She shakes her head. "Not tomorrow. You know it's market day."

"Shoot." I turn to Zig. "Sunday then? Definitely Sunday."

"Definitely definitely? Or definitely maybe?"

"Definitely," I say. He starts down the steps and I head to

the kitchen for lasagna. The smell of Nonna's sauce is pulling me in.

"Gee?" Zig stops on the sidewalk.

"Yeah?"

He points to the bag of leaves he gave me. It's blowing away, flopping down the steps.

"Oh, right!" I trip on Mom's planter and stumble down to grab it. "Thanks!"

I wave and take my leaves inside.

Two down. Twenty-three to go.

CHAPTER 2

Gee! Hey! Hey, Gee! I got a new joke!"

Ian storms down the stairs in his Superman pajamas and almost crashes into me in the kitchen.

"Too early for jokes." I squint into the fridge light looking for last night's leftover lasagna. I bet Dad ate it after Mom went to bed.

"Come on, Gee! Wanna hear a riddle?"

"No." I move a package of tofu, wondering what it's like to live in a house with Pop-Tarts in the cupboard.

"Okay, ready? What do you say when a girl named Gianna wakes up and goes to the bathroom?" He reaches past me and snatches a yogurt.

I try to swat him but miss.

"Give up?" He ducks under my arm and pulls a spoon from the silverware drawer. "You say, 'Gee WHIZ!' Get it, Gee? Gee, WHIZ!"

"Ugh." I pull open the refrigerator drawer where we keep the fruit and almost scream. Balanced on top of the apples is a set of false teeth. They look like they're about to take a big bite.

"Nonna!" I call.

My grandmother hustles into the kitchen and plops her pocketbook on the table. I point into the fridge.

"Oh good. There they are!" She rinses her teeth off under the kitchen faucet and pops them into her mouth.

"Now you . . ." She points a plump finger at Ian. "Let your sister have her breakfast in peace. And you . . ." She raises an eyebrow at my green flannel pajama pants. "You're not even dressed yet. *Sbrigati, sbrigati!*" She claps three times, fast. "Hurry up."

"Ugh." It's 6:30 a.m., and I'm being rushed in old-world Italian.

"Go on." Nonna waves her papery hands in the pink morning sunlight, shooing me upstairs. "It's almost time to leave for the market."

The market became a family ritual when Nonna moved in with us after she broke her hip two years ago. The first Saturday of the month, we pile into the car and cross the border into Canada to shop at the big Italian market in Montreal. Most people think of it as a French city, and it is, but there are all these little pockets of other languages and cultures there, too. There's an English part of the city, a Chinatown, and an Italian section that Nonna says makes her feel like she's home again. It makes her happy. So we go.

By the time I've thrown on my jeans and Picasso T-shirt, everyone else is putting on shoes and jackets. Except Nonna, who's still standing in the kitchen.

"Where did I put my . . . uh . . . my . . ." Nonna taps a finger against her lips. I saw her smile just a minute ago, so I know it's not her teeth again.

Nonna's had trouble remembering the names of things

lately—even plain old ordinary things like brooms and spat-ulas. The other day when she was baking Italian wedding cookies to take to a funeral in the mortuary downstairs, she couldn't remember what her oven mitt was called. She asked us to help find her "hot hand."

I'm starting to worry about her.

"She's just getting older," Mom said when I brought it up last week. "Lord knows you forget things, too . . . like that leaf-collection project you're supposed to be working on." And she sent me to my room to work on it. I made a great col-lage with Nonna's old *National Geographic* magazines instead.

"Come on, Mother! Come on, Gianna! The traffic's going to be worse if we don't hurry!" Mom yells into the kitchen. Nonna's still frowning.

"What did you lose, Nonna?" I ask her.

"My carrying things." She opens the oven door and bends to look inside.

"Your pocketbook?" I pick it up from the kitchen table where she left it ten minutes ago.

"That's it! You're a good girl."

"Smile, Nonna!" Ian leaps into the room with Mom's cell phone camera and snaps her picture.

"Ian?" Mom holds out her hand for the phone. Ian was banned from using it two weeks ago when he jumped out of the shrubs like a member of the paparazzi and ambushed our mailman, who's about eighty years old, with no sense of humor. He snatched the cell phone, marched Ian to the house, and gave Mom a fifteen-minute lecture on parenting. She was embarrassed enough to put Ian on cell phone restriction for life.

Ian drops the phone into Mom's hands and sulks his way out to the other Zalesmobile, the dark green minivan we drive when Dad isn't trying to embarrass me to death.

"Oh, hang on a minute!" I run back to the house for my camera. The market is my favorite place to take pictures; everything there looks so juicy and bright. I pull the door closed and climb into the middle seat next to Nonna. "Okay, ready!"

Dad drives, but Mom's so worried about traffic that she keeps stepping on an imaginary brake on the floor in front of her.

"You know," Dad says after we cross the border into Canada, "I think maybe it's time for a family chat." He does this when we're all held captive in the car.

"How's that leaf collection coming along, Gianna?" Dad tries to catch my eye in the rearview mirror and almost weaves into a Corvette with Quebec plates. Mom swats at him, and he swerves back to his own lane.

"Fine," I say.

"I was talking with Coach the other day when I was waiting to pick you up . . ."

"I know, Dad. No sectionals unless I'm passing science. I know, okay?"

Mom jumps in. "When's the deadline for that leaf project?" Deadlines are her specialty. She does all the bookkeeping and paperwork for the funeral home and is secretary of her women's volunteer group in the community.

"End of next week. We're supposed to have ten leaves by Monday for a start."

"And?" Mom asks.

"And what?" I know I'm being mouthy, but I don't care.

"Mom's trying to help, Gee. We both are. You'd probably like us to *leaf* you alone right now." He winks at me in the rearview mirror. "And we know you're *pining* for the days when you didn't have big projects like this. But you need to get this one finished and *spruced* up by Friday. *Oak*-ay?"

I roll my eyes. "Quit it."

"Sorry." He mirror-winks again. "I was just *needling* you."

I try not to smile. It's hard to stay snotty at Dad. "Well, I think your jokes are way too *sappy*. But I'll get it done. Zig offered to hike with me tomorrow."

"A date?" Nonna perks up. "That Kirby Zigonski is such a nice boy. He's a keeper, Gianna!"

"Nonna!" She wiggles her silver eyebrows at me and I have to laugh. "We're *friends*. He said he'd help me out. But we're *just* friends."

Nonna smirks, like she knows something I don't. The truth is, things have been a little weird with Zig. The other day he was looking at me, and I kept thinking I had spaghetti stuck in my hair or something, but when I asked him what the deal was, he turned reddish and got all busy with his backpack alarm. We've been best friends so long it's just weird to think of him any other way.

"We're *friends,* Nonna," I say again.

"We'll see," she says.

Dad turns up the radio. Mom goes back to balancing the checkbook, with papers and receipts spread out all over her lap. I can look out the window in peace.

I love to watch how things change when we drive into the city. Condominiums are the first signs that Montreal's getting close. They're built up along the St. Lawrence River, thicker and thicker until you get to the bridge. It's named after the explorer Jacques Cartier, but Dad calls it "the ol' Jack Carter Bridge" to bug Mom. She thinks everything should be pronounced properly.

Traffic isn't bad, so fifteen minutes past the bridge, we pull into the big parking lot for the market. I complain about getting up early on Saturdays, but I love this place. It's like jumping into a giant tossed salad—fruits and vegetables and flowers of every color. People of every color, too. You can walk around and sample cheese from Quebec goats, crunchy apples, tangy dried cranberries. There's a store that just sells olive oil—about a million different kinds. One bottle costs five hundred dollars! Every time we go in there, I wonder what it must taste like. They never offer samples of that one.

Today, Nonna needs a big jug of regular, normally priced olive oil, so she picks out her favorite kind and chats in Italian with the old man at the counter while he puts the jug in a paper sack. Mom and Dad have gone to pick up a bottle of wine. I'm checking out all the different shapes of bottles while I try to keep Ian from destroying them. I love the lines in the bottles, the way they overlap one another, the way some bottles have big loopy handles. This would be a great place to sit and draw, but I left my sketchbook in the car.

Ian and I follow Nonna out into the crisp air. The smell of fall leaves mixes with hot apple cider someone is serving from a cart.

"Want some?" Nonna asks.

"No thanks. I want my hands free for pictures." She buys Ian a cup while I unzip my camera case and snap a few pictures of the vegetable vendors as we pass. Maybe I'll draw one of these scenes later.

So many colors get thrown together here, like they're all shouting to be heard at once. Orange pumpkins next to bright pink mums with dark green leaves. Yellow gourds piled high next to crates of polished red apples. I'm clicking away when Ian pulls on my sleeve.

"Nonna went over there to get some eggplant. You're in charge of me." He grins and dribbles cider down the front of his shirt. "She says she'll meet us in the bakery when you're done."

The bakery isn't just any bakery. It's the greatest bakery in the universe. The best thing about market Saturdays is when we all meet there for the last stop of the day. There's a glass case full of desserts that look like they were clipped out of food magazines. My favorite is the Royale. *"Une Royale, s'il vous plaît,"* is how I order it, since the bakery staff only speaks French. If I get it right, I end up with a perfect little rectangle of dense cake layered with fluffy mousse. It's like eating a chocolate cloud.

I'm hungry just thinking about it, so I put away my camera and take Ian's hand. Mom and Dad are walking up to the bakery door too.

"Nonna's grabbing an eggplant," I tell them.

"Mmmm." Mom licks her lips. "Is she making eggplant parmesan tonight?"

"She didn't say."

Ian snatches Mom's cell phone back from her purse while she's busy thinking about eggplant. A burly man in a blue flannel shirt opens the door for us.

"Merci." Mom steps inside. Ian snaps his picture.

The smell of the bread almost lifts me off the floor. How do people work here all day and not eat everything? I'd constantly be sticking my fingers in the frosting and licking them.

Mom takes a number and waits for them to call it. I try to tune out the bustling feet of the crowds, the clinking of coins in the cash register, and listen for our number. It's my first year of French class in school, and we've already done numbers, but Madame Wilder speaks slowly and clearly when she's teaching us. Here, French words just fly out of people's mouths like barn swallows. I have to listen hard or our number flits past before I can blink.

"Trente-huit?" The woman behind the counter looks around and I think hard. Thirty-eight. That's us! Mom nods at me and I step forward to try our order: two baguettes, three cream-filled éclairs, a fruit tart for Nonna, and my royal chocolate cake. I may not have studied the body parts, but I did look up all my favorite food words and practice the order at home last night so I could get it right.

"Je voudrais deux baguettes, s'il vous plaît. Aussi trois éclairs de la crème, une tarte de fruits, et une Royale." I search the woman's face to see if she knows what I mean. Mom nudges me and I remember to add *"S'il vous plaît,"* which means "please."

The bakery lady smiles at me and starts putting things in a box. Apparently, I've done all right. I turn around so Nonna can congratulate me and realize that she hasn't met us yet.

"Shouldn't Nonna be done by now?" I ask Mom. "The eggplant guy is only a few booths away."

"She's probably chatting up Mr. Passini." Mom's ogling the croissants, but they're made with so much butter she never lets herself have one. She checks her watch. "We should be leaving soon. Go see if you can hurry her along."

I'd rather wait for our bakery order and maybe rip off a hunk of bread to sample, but I grab Ian's arm and pull him toward the door.

"Smile!" He clicks a shot of the bakery staff on his way out.

When we get to the booth where Nonna buys her eggplant, Mr. Passini is there with his cocker spaniel.

"Ah, *come stai,* Gianna?"

"Bene, grazie, e tu?" I tell him I'm well and ask how he is. That's about as far as I can go on the Italian that Nonna's taught me, though. Mr. Passini understands.

"Just fine. Your grandmother hasn't found you yet?"

"We thought she'd be here."

"No, we were out of eggplant, so I sent her to Hassan." He points to the next row of vegetable sellers, past a display of cornstalks and pumpkins.

"Thanks." Ian snaps a photo of Mr. Passini waving.

"Grazie!" I try to grab the phone from Ian, but he's too quick. "Quit it! Mom's going to be mad." He follows me across the aisle.

"But I like taking pictures, so I can remember important stuff." He holds the phone up to get a shot of some rutabagas.

Hassan, it turns out, still has eggplant and tells us Nonna left with one of them about fifteen minutes ago. She should have met us at the bakery.

Ian and I walk up and down the aisles looking for Nonna until we end up in a big booth bursting with pumpkins. She's not here either, so we start up the last row of vendors.

My heart's pumping faster, and my stomach feels all tight. What if she fell? What if it's her hip again, or worse?

I look at the cell phone in Ian's hand and wish Nonna had one that we could call.

"Let's go find Mom and Dad," I decide, pulling him away from a plate of pineapple samples. A car horn blasts on the street next to us and makes me jump. When I look, I see an old lady scurrying out of the way of a delivery truck. A man in a green wool hat shouts something in another language from the driver's window. When the truck passes, the woman is standing at the side of the street. She looks scared and confused. Wisps of gray hair drift out from under her scarf, and one of her shoes is untied. She looks down the alley one way and then looks up toward the bakery, like she can't remember where she is or where she's supposed to be. Her jacket hangs over one arm. In her other arm, she's cradling an eggplant.

"Nonna!" Ian pulls away from me and runs across the street without checking for cars. When I catch up, Nonna is already shaking her finger at him, warning about city traffic.

"What happened?" I ask her. She still looks confused, and somehow, it makes me a little angry. I want her to tie her shoe and fix her hair.

"I picked up the eggplant and then I couldn't find my car," she says, looking toward the parking lot. "I thought I parked on the street, but maybe not."

"Nonna, we drove the van, and we parked in the lot. You were supposed to meet us at the bakery. Remember?" How could she have forgotten the bakery?

My heart is still thumping from our search through the market, and here she is wandering around with her eggplant. How could she not remember to show up at the bakery?

"Of course." Nonna's mouth forms a tight grin, and she

fakes knocking herself on the head. "Now I remember." But I'm not sure I believe her.

Mom and Dad walk up with long French bread in a paper bag and a bakery box tied with blue ribbon. "There you are, Mom. Are we all set now?" she asks Nonna.

"She got lost, Mom." I try to tell her about Hassan and the delivery truck, but she just puts her hand on Nonna's shoulder. Dad takes the eggplant from her and holds her elbow when we step up on the curb.

"It *is* awfully busy here today." Mom pats Nonna's shoulder again. "It's tough to find anyone in this crowd."

"Hey, look," Dad says, holding up Nonna's eggplant so the stem sticks out like a nose. Above it are two dents like squinting eyes. "Doesn't this sort of look like Mr. Passini?" Dad wiggles the eggplant so it looks like it's talking.

"Hello, Gianna," Mr. Eggplant-Passini says as Dad bobs his head up and down. "You're looking lovely today. Are you having me with olive oil or marinara sauce tonight?"

Nonna shakes her head, laughing, and takes her eggplant back.

On the drive south, we talk about Italian recipes and French pastries, fancy olive oil and when we'll carve our pumpkins for Halloween.

But I keep remembering the look on the face of that old lady across the street. She had no idea where she was. And it scared her.

CHAPTER 3

When we get home, Mom won't talk about Nonna getting lost. I try to bring it up while we're making the salad.

"Mom—you should have seen her." I slice the cucumber into the bowl and reach for a potato chip from the bag Dad bought at the market when Mom wasn't looking.

"Put that down," Mom says. "Do you know how much trans fat is in those?"

Mom tosses the chips into the trash. Dad walks by and gazes in at them like he's saying good-bye to an old friend.

"Don't you have a French quiz coming up? Have you studied?" Mom asks. She points to her elbow. "What's this?"

"It's your elbow." I start slicing a second cucumber.

"*En français,* Gianna!"

I have no clue what her elbow is in French, and even if I did, I can't concentrate. "Mom . . . ," I try again. "Nonna had no idea where she was."

"So she was confused for a minute." She scoops up the salad bowl before I'm done slicing and whisks it over to the table.

"But she was standing there in the middle of the—"

"It's a big market, and it could have happened to anyone.

You forget things too. Now go wash your hands and come sit down."

We eat our eggplant parmesan in silence.

Sunday morning, I wake up to Zig's special knock and shuffle downstairs in my Big Bird slippers to unlock the door.

"Come on in." I lead him toward the kitchen. "I think everybody's eating. I'm the last one up."

"Is that my future grandson-in-law?" Nonna calls. When we walk in, she gives Zig her biggest smile and puts down her rolling pin. "I'm going to make these cookies for your wedding someday, you know."

She's rolling dough between her palms, shaping little round cookies for later. The first batch is already cooling on the counter. Her eyes twinkle at us. "What do you think, you two? Will you want them with sprinkles or powdered sugar? Go ahead and try both. Then you can decide."

"Nonna!" My face feels like I'm standing too close to the open oven door. She's always joked about how I ought to marry Zig, but never in front of him. Geez!

"Uh . . . I think I'll just have a muffin," Zig mumbles, and shuffles over to the table, looking at his feet the whole time.

I look at Nonna with big cut-it-out eyes, but she just smirks again. I take a cookie, even though I'm annoyed with her.

Nonna makes the best Italian wedding cookies in the world, even if they aren't really served up at weddings. At our house, Nonna's cookies usually end up being funeral cookies. She always brings them when Dad has calling hours scheduled downstairs. Whether she knows the family of the dead person or not, Nonna shows up with a big plate of cookies.

She says food holds sweet memories, and those memories help people say good-bye.

"Hey, Zig!" Ian looks up from his riddle book with jam on his face. "Why did the cookie stay home from school?"

"I give up. Why?"

"Because it was feeling crummy! Get it? Crumby?" Ian laughs so hard, toast crumbs spray out of his mouth. Zig smiles and hands him a napkin.

"Morning, Mr. Zales."

Dad nods from behind his coffee. "Helping Gee with her leaf project?" He points to a plate of Nonna's apple crumb muffins on the table.

"Yep—twenty-five leaves by Friday." Zig reaches for a muffin. "And I have the perfect idea for helping her remember the kinds of leaves." He turns to me. "We should change the dog game to the tree game for the next week."

"The dog game?" Dad asks.

"It's a game we started a couple of years ago, where we assign everybody a dog," I tell him.

"Like the kind of dog they'd have for a pet?"

"No, the kind of dog they would *be* if they were a dog," Zig tells him. "Take me, for example. I'm a border collie."

I nod. "Shaggy hair, super intelligent, and a loyal companion." Zig smiles, proud to be a border collie.

"And you?" Dad looks at me.

"Irish setter. The American Kennel Club says I'm friendly and amusing."

"I won't argue with that." Dad sneaks a cookie while Nonna's rinsing the mixing bowl. "Have you assigned me a dog yet?"

Zig gives me a sideways look, and I try hard not to laugh.

"Well?" Dad puts his hands on his hips.

"Basset hound," Zig says. "Sorry."

Dad's gaze drops to the gut hanging over his belt, and he frowns. "Come on."

"You have to admit . . ." I pat him on the belly. He puts his cookie back.

"I don't think I like the dog game."

"That's okay because the dog game just became the tree game," Zig proclaims. "Same thing, only with trees." He points to me. "You're a sugar maple because they're colorful and fluttery. I'm . . ."

"You're that big tall brown tree in front of the school!" I get it now.

"The oak?" Zig says. "Why am I an oak?"

"Because you're not all showy. But you're important, and . . . stable."

Zig taps his chin with his finger. "Okay." He nods. "I'm an oak. But I want to be a red oak. White oak leaves are all loopy and weird looking."

"Fine," I tell him. "Hold on . . . I'll be right down after I get dressed."

"I thought we'd hike Great Bear Mountain," Zig calls up after me.

"Sounds good. Is your mom waiting for us in the car?" I ask from upstairs.

"Nope," Zig answers. "She had to work. I figured we could bike there."

"Bike!" I come downstairs and expect to see the I'm-just-kidding look on his face. Nope.

"It's only eight miles."

. . .

Only eight miles.

Ha.

It may be eight miles, but the eight miles from our house to the trailhead are not regular miles. They're eight miles up and down every hill in the Green Mountains. Running didn't prepare me for this. By the time Zig and I get to the trailhead, my mouth feels like I've just eaten a full bag of cotton balls. I sucked up every drop from my water bottle in the first five miles.

Zig catches his breath first. "Ready to hike?"

I wipe my face on the shoulder of my T-shirt and hope my cheeks aren't hideously red. It's bad enough that half my hair has escaped from its ponytail and is curling out in frizzy little explosions around my ears. I wonder what kind of tree has scraggly edges and shiny cheeks.

By the time I catch up to Zig, he's already stopped at a tree with low branches, squinting up at the leaves through his thick glasses. They're held together on the side with duct tape again.

"Zig." I point to the sticky gray mass of tape. "You look like a bad cartoon of a nerd."

"This will be in style soon. I'm a trendsetter." He laughs and pushes up the glasses. "Besides, frames are expensive." I look down at my sneakers. Zig's dad left before I met him, and his mom works two jobs.

"Here." Zig pushes the leaf key into my hands. "You follow the key and ask me the questions, and I'll let you know which answer to go with."

I ask, he answers, and I turn to whatever page the book says to go to. It's pretty easy.

"Okay, are the leaves simple or compound?" I try to sound official.

"Simple."

"That doesn't look simple to me." I frown and look over his shoulder at what appears to be a pretty fancy leaf.

"They're simple." He elbows me back onto the trail. "That means they're not compound—with more than one blade attached to a single stalk. Remember?"

I nod, even though I don't. The leaf key says turn to page 4.

"Are they alternate or opposite?"

"Opposite."

"Opposite of what?"

Zig sighs. "Each other. They're across from each other on the same twig." He points to the spot on the branch where they're attached.

"Okay, hold on." I try to flip to page 6 like it says, but I end up dropping the booklet. It lands at the edge of a puddle.

"Sorry." I rescue it and wipe the mud onto my shorts. Zig says the leaves have five lobes with a palmate arrangement, smooth edges with few teeth, and rounded sinuses, whatever that means, so I turn to page 9.

"Okay, when you break the stalk that connects the leaf blade to the twig, is there a milky sap?"

"Let's see." Zig snaps off a whole branch so he can see more clearly, and I lean in to check for sap. My cheek brushes against his shoulder, and he jumps back as if I've shocked him.

I step forward again, careful to stay in my own space this time. "Any milky sap?" I ask hopefully.

"No." He frowns and seems sad about this.

"Are you sure?" I squint at the leaf. No sap, milky or otherwise. Maybe he did it wrong. "Try another leaf."

"Nope, no milky sap there either."

"Huh."

"Gianna?"

"Yeah?"

"The key?"

"What?"

"The key. What does the key say if there's no milky sap?"

"Oh!" I forgot about the key. It didn't occur to me that we could go on without milky sap, but we're in luck. We can turn to page 12.

"Do the leaves have five lobes without a downy underside, or three lobes with a downy underside?"

"Five. Not downy."

"Okay." The guide says to go to page 16 now, and I'm wondering just how long this is going to go on. Maybe we're on one of those reality TV shows, and it's just going to keep having us turn pages all afternoon, with people watching from a hidden camera to see how long we'll stay at it. I turn to page 16, and finally, there are no more questions.

"It's a sugar maple!" I yell. I do a little maple dance to celebrate. "A sugar maple! We found a sugar maple!"

"Cool." Zig takes two plastic Baggies from his backpack and puts a sugar maple leaf inside of each. He labels the bags with a permanent marker and hands me one.

"Thanks," I say. "Phew! I guess we can get moving now." I tuck the leaf and the guide into my backpack and climb on up the hill, leaves crunching under my feet.

"Gee?"

"Yeah?" I feel much better now that our leaf is identified.

"You still need to collect and identify twenty-two more leaves."

It's going to be a long afternoon.

. . .

It takes us three hours to reach the summit of what's usually a forty-five-minute hill, and I'm happy enough to cheer when I finally see the sky open up over the tree line. I stop for a second to take in the gentle curves of the hills below us, the flat mirror of Lake Champlain beyond, the Adirondacks looming, purplish gray on the other side.

"Over here." Zig points to a flat stretch of rock next to a craggy pine tree.

By the time we plop down on the warm rock, we've identified a grand total of six leaves. Out of twenty-five.

"This is child abuse," I whine. Zig pulls a big bag of M&M'S from his backpack and rips it open. He shakes a bunch into his hand, picks out the blue ones, which he's done ever since he read *Chasing Vermeer,* funnels the rest into the bag, and hands it to me. I take a big fistful of rainbow colors and pop them into my mouth all at once.

"We've already had two weeks to work on it, though," Zig says through blue lips. "This last-minute stuff kills you, Gee. How come you always do this to yourself?"

"I don't know." I sigh and lean back on the flat rock. I close my eyes, and the sun beats right through them so I see red. It could be August, it feels so warm today, but October in Vermont can be tricky. One minute, you're sunbathing, and the next minute, it starts snowing like crazy.

"It's not that I don't plan to do the work." I open my eyes and pick at some moss growing out of a crack in the rock. "It's just that I'm always busy with cross-country and stuff. Then when it gets to be almost the due date, and things are . . . well . . . urgent, I get all stressed out."

I've made a little mound of crumbly dry moss hair on the

rock. Zig puts his hand over mine and frowns. "Stop picking at that," he says. "It's protected."

"The moss is an endangered species or something?" I laugh. The laugh comes out funny, though. My hand is all tingly, where his warm hand covers it. Maybe my hands are just cold. Before I can figure it out, his hand is gone. I guess he was only worried about the moss.

"It's not endangered, exactly, but it's protected. It only grows in an alpine habitat, which only exists at the tops of mountains around here. This one, too." He scoots over a few rocks and points to a delicate pink flower with dusty leaves that seems to be growing right out of the rock. Amazing.

I lean down to smell the flower but can't catch any scent. I run my fingers over the smooth rock where its leaves are resting, all gray and feathery.

When I look up, Zig is leaning over a different rock, with his forehead almost touching it. "Check this out." He waves me over. I squat down next to him but can't see what he's looking at.

"Isn't it awesome?" He leans in closer.

"Well, it's a nice rock. Kind of like that one I was sitting on over there before you called me over here. They're all really nice rocks, I guess."

"No." He motions me in closer. "Look."

I scrunch way down and squint at the rock like he's doing, and then I see it. Tiny little seashells in the stone. Ocean shells. On top of a mountaintop that feels like it's miles in the sky. I look up and see Zig's grin.

"They're fossils. From when this whole valley used to be

part of the ocean, millions of years ago, before the mountains formed."

I run my fingers over the lines of the fossils and feel like I haven't been around very long.

A flock of Canada geese flies past, heading south along the lake, honking like crazy. They sound like they're arguing about which way to go.

Honk, honk! No, we were supposed to take a left at that tall mountain back there!

A left?! Honk! I thought it was a right.

When the geese grow quiet and so small I can't see their wings flapping anymore, Zig starts packing up.

"Let's go. It's going to get dark, and we want to head down while there's still enough light to collect leaves."

I put the empty M&M'S bag in my backpack and take a last look over all the shades of red and gold. It feels like I could fly off the mountain, leap onto one of those patches of color, and land like I'm on Nonna's big patchwork quilt over the down mattress.

The rocks don't feel like Nonna's quilt, though. As usual, I try to go too fast and fall on the way down. I land at the base of a tree with smooth brown bark and kind of striped leaves.

"Hey!" I shout to Zig. "We don't have this one yet!"

"It's an American beech." He barely looks at the leaves.

"What about the key? How do you know?"

"Don't need a key for this one." He pulls down a branch so I can reach to pluck off two leaves. "When Grampa was alive, he used to take me out to his camp, and we'd see these all over. They're the last trees to lose their leaves in the winter. You see, none have fallen yet." He points to the ground at the base of the tree, bare and brown except for a few bright red maple leaves that have blown over, another tree's litter scattered in the wind. "Stubborn old tree."

"Nonna," I say, rubbing a sturdy leaf between my fingers.

"Huh?"

"It's a Nonna tree."

Zig nods. "Nonna's an American beech for sure. And here's the best part." He bends down to pick up a small brown nut. "Beechnuts."

"Do you eat them?"

"People don't usually eat them." He smiles. "But bears love them."

"Not here." I laugh. "Bears don't hang out this close to the main road."

"No?" Zig smiles. "Then who do you suppose did that?" He points to a spot on the tree about two feet above my head, where four deep claw marks have left trails in the bark. How big would a bear have to be to reach up that high with his claws? And more importantly, if he's the one who made all these nuts fall at our feet, when is he coming back for his snack?

"Let's go!" I grab Zig's sleeve and give a quick tug before I start off stumbling down the hill again.

"Slow down. Bears won't be out now with all the noise you're making. And besides, you miss all the good stuff when you go that fast."

Zig puts out an arm to stop me. Dry leaves rustle in front of our feet.

"Look," he whispers.

A black-and-gold garter snake stretches out on the rock in

the sun about three feet in front of us. I would have stepped right on him. His warm, shiny scales gleam smooth and black as the marble counter in our bathroom. His eyes are beads of glass, and his tongue flicks out so long and thin, it's like a needle tasting the air. We stand and watch for a minute before I try to take one step to get just a little closer. When I do, the snake pulls itself off the rock into the leaves at the side of the trail. The point of his tail is the last to disappear into a pile of yellow-brown leaves that I recognize.

"Paper-tree leaves." I scoop up a few. They're damp underneath and smell like the earth when I hold them to my nose.

"It's a birch." Zig looks up at the tree's cool white bark.

"I know. We had one in the yard when I was little, and I used to peel off the bark and draw on it." I reach out to touch a little piece of bark that's peeling off the tree and squint at the sun setting through its leaves. Some of the branches are drooping so low they almost touch the ground, so it's easy for me to grab a couple of leaves and add them to my collection. I drop my backpack and jump up to catch a branch that's just begging me to hang on it for a minute.

"Gianna Z." Zig looks up and smiles. "Swinger of birches."

"Huh?" I cross my eyes at him, get swinging, and flip a leg over the branch so I'm sitting on it. It dips lower but doesn't break.

"'Swinger of Birches.' It's a Robert Frost poem in our English book. I read ahead."

"Of course you did." I drop a leaf in his hair.

He picks up my backpack and holds it out, singing that song that starts with all the leaves being brown. It's "California Dreamin'." And it's way off-key.

Zig holds out a hand to help me jump down, and I take my bag from him. It gets dark fast when the sun sinks behind the trees. "Ready?"

"Ready." I start to rush down but change my mind and wait for him to walk alongside me the last half mile out of the woods. I can't help but think about those claw marks on the beech tree. If a bear comes along, I'd like to have some protection. If nothing else, I bet Zig's singing would scare it off.

CHAPTER 4

Monday.

Ugh.

It's a gray morning. A roll-over-and-snuggle-deeper-in-the-covers morning. I studied for the French quiz a little last night, so I can officially complain that my *jambes*—that means "legs"—are killing me from the bike ride.

Plus, I still don't have all my leaves for today's deadline.

I flop over, and Miranda, my stuffed panda, slips over the edge of the loft into the Garbage Pit. That's what Mom calls the space under my bed that was supposed to be my study area. I turned it into an art studio instead, with a small table and plastic containers for my pencils, oil pastels, paints, and brushes. It's awesome, but it's messy and sometimes a little sticky down there when I'm in the middle of something, which is always. I hope Miranda didn't land in wet paint.

My alarm goes off again. I lean up onto my elbow, peek over the edge of my loft, and pull back the orange curtains that Nonna made for me when I wanted to paint my walls orange and Mom said no. She said that would be silly and nobody has orange walls and how would we ever sell the house. I pointed out that we weren't moving, but it didn't matter. I got boring white walls and curtains the color of pumpkins to sort of make up for it.

I look out the window, hoping for lightning or a tornado or some other good reason not to run, but it looks fine. Cold and cloudy, but fine.

Bianca's probably out training by now, a voice in my head says.

Shut up, I tell the voice.

But I climb down from my loft anyway.

Miranda's okay. She landed in a pile of magazine clippings I'm saving for a new collage. They probably helped break her fall. I pick her up and toss her into the heap of stuffed animals balanced against the wall under the window. They have to stay all piled up there because they're covering up splashes of paint from the Jackson Pollock splatter painting I tried to do. I was really careful. I put down garbage bags on the floor before I started splattering and everything. Who knew that paint on a twirling eggbeater would go so far? I'm sure Miranda will be happy to help hide the evidence.

I get dressed fast because once I get going, I'll be glad I went out. Running always wakes me up. And I need those leaves anyway.

"Morning, Gee!" Ian's at the table with a bowl of Cheerios. He's trying to eat them out of an ice-cream scoop, and milk is dribbling down his chin. "Wanna hear a riddle?"

"No." I open the fridge to grab my water bottle. No teeth in there today. But the book Nonna was reading last night is leaning against the milk.

"Okay, ready . . . Knock-knock . . ."

"Who's there?" I sit down on the steps to tie my running shoes.

"Sarah."

"Sarah who?" I zip my sweatshirt.

"Sarah doctor in the house? Because the way you look first thing in the morning is making me sick!"

He laughs so hard he almost chokes on his Cheerios and probably goes on laughing long after I slam the door.

I take a deep breath and jog down the driveway. The air feels like little needles pricking into my lungs, but it's a good cold—a wake-up kind of cold—and when I exhale, my breath makes puffy white clouds in front of my face.

"Hi, Mrs. Warren!" I call across the street, where my neighbor has stepped out in her pajamas to get the newspaper. "I really like that tree in your front yard. Do you know what kind it is?"

"Why yes!" She looks up at it, pleased. "It's a Japanese maple." So is she, I decide. She's ornamental and decorative in her pink flowered nightshirt and satin pajama pants. She takes her paper inside, and I dart up onto the lawn to snatch a leaf.

At the corner, I pass Mr. Webster, the old man whose heart surgeon told him last summer that he has to go for a walk every day to get some exercise.

"Morning, Miss Zales," he says, and I wave and slow down a little. He's an oak, like Zig.

But there's no Zig yet today. Just old Mr. Webster.

"Mr. Webster, do you know what this tree is with the really huge leaves and the long pods?"

"Catalpa!" He shouts because he has trouble hearing and

thinks everyone else does too. I grab one of the leaves that's fallen in the road and keep running.

Catalpa, catalpa. Japanese maple and catalpa. I have the key to identify them later, but this way I'll be sure.

I pull my hands inside my sleeves and look up at the streetlight. A few sparkly little snowflakes are starting to fall. October snow!

When I was younger, I used to hate it if we had snow before Halloween because Mom would make me wear a huge puffy coat over my costume. One year, a giant puke-green parka swallowed my princess dress. I love early snow now, though. Especially snow that happens when you least expect it and just sprinkles down for a little while. It feels like a secret.

Zig would love this. I wonder if he's running late.

I turn the next corner. No Zig. But the snowflakes get bigger. They're the huge, fluffy ones that fall slowly like little white parachutes. I open my mouth, hoping some will fall in, but they all seem to land on my cheeks instead. I figure out I have to aim better, so I start watching individual flakes, tracking them on the way down so I can be in the right place when they get to mouth level. Weaving back and forth and ducking once in a while, I manage to catch five flakes on my tongue. They taste like Christmas.

I look down in time to swerve so I don't crash into Mr. Nelson and Mr. Collins walking their dogs. They've lived in the blue house on the corner as long as anyone can remember. They're both amazing piano players, and if you walk by their house at night in the summertime when the windows are open, you can almost always hear music.

What kind of tree is friendly and musical? I'll have to check with Zig later.

"Hey, Mr. Nelson, do you know what kind of tree this is?" I jog up and point at a tree with feathery leaves. The dogs lunge forward and growl. They're Pomeranians—like fluffy white rats, only louder. They pull at their leashes and snarl like pit bulls every day when I run by, and every time, Mr. Nelson gasps in surprise.

"Care Bear! Snuggles! What's gotten into you?" he says as he pulls the dogs away from me and looks up at his tree. "It's a Kentucky coffee tree. Isn't it a beauty?"

"Yeah," I say.

"No, it's not." Mr. Collins squints up at the tree and frowns. "That's a honey locust."

"No, James, that's a Kentucky coffee tree. I remember that nice realtor lady, Bertha Jane Hemingway, telling us about it when she sold us the house."

"Well, Bertha Jane Hemingway lied, because that's not a Kentucky coffee tree."

"It most certainly is. And Bertha Jane would absolutely flip her wig if she heard you say that."

"That she lied? Or that it's not a coffee tree?"

"Well, both, probably."

"Well, she better get flipping, because it's a honey locust, and she lied if she told you anything else. Come on, Care Bear." He takes the leash and walks off down the sidewalk.

"Honestly . . ." Mr. Nelson pulls a few leaves from the tree and hands them to me. "Kentucky coffee tree," he whispers. "Write it down."

I nod and wave as he and Snuggles run to catch up. I'll double-check it in my book later.

Now it's snowing really hard—hard enough that my sweat-shirt gets coated with a feathery layer of white that I have to brush off every few minutes. It's so quiet, except for my sneakers thumping dark prints into the new snow. I tip my head up to watch the big flakes drift in the streetlights. This was worth getting up for.

I look down again and there's Zig. Hopping off his bike with his newspaper bag about five houses up ahead. He jogs up and leaves the folded paper between the storm door and the screen, where Mrs. Donaldson likes it. He jumps back on his bike and coasts past me with a big smile.

I lift a quick hand to wave and keep running. We don't say anything, not even hello. It's an unspoken rule we have. We both love mornings because of the quiet. Maybe we'll talk about the secret snow later, and maybe not. But I like know-ing Zig saw it, too.

When I turn the corner for home, the snow starts to let up a little, and I spot another runner up ahead about half a block. Her pink running shorts barely cover her *derriere,* as Madame Wilder would say.

My legs must have their own brains because they decide all by themselves to speed up. A lot. Until I'm running right alongside her.

"Morning, Bianca!" I shout so she can't help but hear me even through the iPod buds stuck in her ears.

She startles, and it breaks her stride, so I put on a new burst of speed and push past her. "See ya!" I call over my shoulder and run right past my house and around the corner again. Even though I really need to get showered to be on time for school. Even though another lap around the block will make me late. Even though that little stunt with Bianca will cost me later when she's surrounded by her fan club in the cafeteria.

Sometimes running feels too good to stop.

I only do one more lap, though. I turn the corner and slow to a jog to cool down. Up ahead, I can see the blur of Bianca's pink shorts as she crosses the street. It looks like she's sped up, which is weird since she ought to be at the end of her run, too.

But then I see why.

Care Bear is loose. He's chasing Bianca, snapping at her heels like he thinks he's a Doberman.

Maybe today won't be so bad after all.

CHAPTER 5

I shower as fast as I can, and I'm ready on time, but now I can't find my backpack.

"Nonna, have you seen my backpack?"

"The red one?"

"No, that was, like, in third grade when I had a red one. It's blue—dark blue with those silver moons on it. You know . . ."

"I always liked that red one." She puts her tea in the microwave to heat it up and opens the oven door to peek in. "Not in here," she says.

I check the hall closet.

"Dad, will you help me look?"

"Where did you last see it?" Dad asks, looking up from his casket catalog. This makes me want to kill him, so I have to stop looking and tell him so.

"If I knew where I last saw it, don't you think I'd be there right now looking for it instead of running around the house at random?"

"Did you take it on your hike?" Dad flips to a page of mahogany caskets and sips coffee from his travel mug like he has all the time in the world.

"Actually, yes!" I forgive him for the where-did-you-last-see-it routine when I remember I left it in the garage with my bike. It's there, hanging from the handlebars, so I grab it and head outside for the van. Except the van's gone.

"Mom had an early meeting, so it's you and me." Dad tilts his head toward the hearse. "Besides, I have to pick up Mr. Disilvio at ten."

"Dad! Not again!"

"Come on." Dad opens the door for me. I slide into the passenger seat and turn on the radio. The digital clock says 7:48. Nine minutes to get to school. Two for my locker, and one to navigate through the crowd to homeroom and listen to Bianca's new cadaver jokes. I might make it.

I unzip my backpack to start shoving in binders and find the bag of leaves from the hike. I add the new ones I got this morning and put the bag on the seat behind me so the leaves don't get crushed while I organize my binders.

"How's the leaf collection coming now?" Dad eyes my leaf bag in the rearview mirror.

"Pretty good." I pull an orange from the bottom of my bag. It's soft and leaking some kind of sticky syrup. I toss that in back, too. "Zig and I got a bunch of leaves on our hike, and I just need to do some research on them this week so I can put the whole thing together."

"Have you told Coach you're getting caught up?" We're at a red light, so Dad turns to face me. "You know, she may have to send someone else to sectionals unless—"

"She's *not* sending someone else. I'll have it done, *okay*?" I pretend I'm still arranging my binders. We've had this conversation about homework and grades and projects about a million times.

I do all the readings and I do all the homework. It's just that somehow, when Mrs. Loring gives us those multiple-choice questions with the little bubbles to fill in, more than one answer seems like a good idea to me. I'm not a one-bubble kind of girl.

"Okay." Dad stretches and puts his hand on my shoulder as we pull to a stop in the circle in front of the school's main office. "Happy Monday."

"Thanks." I lean over, kiss him on the cheek, sling my backpack over my shoulder, and grab the leaf book that fell out onto the seat. I hop out of the car before he can say anything else about leaves. Almost.

"Hey, wait!" he calls.

"Yeah?"

"You never told me about that tree game."

"What about it?"

"Did you decide about me?"

"Umm . . ." The bell is about to ring, and I haven't used the leaf guide enough to decide what a Dad-tree would be. I flip through the book until I find a short tree that's kind of chubby and droopy. "How about a dwarf mulberry?" I blow him a kiss.

"Hmph." Dad puts the car in gear as I slam the door. Clearly, he was hoping to be a redwood.

I just make it to homeroom, catch my breath during the announcements, wait for the bell, and make another mad dash down the hall for first-period English. I sink into a chair and pull out my assignment notebook to make sure I have my homework for the day.

Reading letter for English class. Check. It's right here in the assignment book.

Math problems 2 through 14 (evens) on page 152. Check. That's in my math binder.

Review parts of body for French quiz. Check.

Science Leaf Project—Collect first ten leaves by October 7th. Check. The bag's right here in my backpack. I move the binders aside and plunge my hand to the bottom. Aside from some leftover orange stickiness, there's nothing. I take out the binders, one by one, until the backpack is empty.

Crud. My leaves are in the back of the hearse. And I can't call Dad. He's picking up Rudy Disilvio's body.

I hope Mr. Disilvio likes nature.

After I turn in my reading letter—the homework that I didn't lose—I pull a new pencil from my backpack and reach for my sketchbook.

The pencil rolls off my desk and over toward Ruby Kinsella. She slouches down in her seat so she can reach it with her foot and kicks it back to me.

"Thanks," I whisper. Ruby peeks out from under a thin curtain of wispy blond hair and smiles. She's a weeping willow, quiet and breezy and nice.

I settle in to draw while Mrs. Clancy passes out papers. I sketch a beech-tree leaf, like the ones Zig and I saw on Sunday.

I pencil in its rough, ragged edges. A gust of wind rattles the window, and I look out. Leaves are whooshing all over the place, flying past horizontally as if they have engines of their own.

I watch them fly for a minute and sigh. They're all going to be rotting in a drainage ditch before I can collect the rest of my twenty-five. If I could choose a magical power, I'd want the power to freeze time so I could keep those leaves right where they are, finish my project, and take my time about it.

I draw the deep lines that go from the center of the beech leaf to its edges and remember how strong it looked, holding on in the wind. A Nonna leaf.

If I could, I'd freeze time for Nonna, too. I'd go back in time a year—even six months would do it. Back to the days when she knew her way around the market and remembered where she left her purse. It used to feel like Nonna would be with us forever. She never felt old to me until now.

Saturday freaked me out. It's happening more and more; she just sort of drifts away for a while. She comes back, but there are times when I don't even think she hears me when I'm talking. I guess I shouldn't blame her for that. I get yelled at for daydreaming in class at least three times a day. I always come back too.

"Gianna, can you tell us who wrote this poem?" I look up from my drawing to Mrs. Clancy's whiteboard and see the title "Birches."

"Birches"? Zig talked about this poem!

"Robert Frost." I recover from my daydream in time to answer.

"Very good." She shows us a picture of an old man with white hair, more wrinkles than I can count, and eyes droopier than a basset hound's. Then she starts reading.

> *"When I see birches bend to left and right*
> *Across the lines of straighter darker trees,*
> *I like to think some boy's been swinging them."*

She keeps reading, but I stop there to check out the picture. This guy looks about ninety years old and grumpy too. What could he possibly know about climbing trees? I have to skip a few lines to catch up with Mrs. Clancy's reading. The narrator talks about how ice storms are probably the real reason the birches are bent over. That I understand. Two years ago, an ice storm knocked out our power for three days, and when it was all over, we had to take down two birch trees that never stood back up. I like this poem, so I catch up again.

"But I was going to say when Truth broke in
With all her matter of fact about the ice storm,
I should prefer to have some boy bend them
As he went out and in to fetch the cows—
Some boy too far from town to learn baseball,
Whose only play was what he found himself,
Summer or winter, and could play alone."

This part reminds me of Zig, so I doodle his name in the margin of my notebook. He'll spend hours out in his yard just puttering around, making slingshots and wiring up alarms for his fort. The kid in the poem spends his time climbing birch trees, really carefully, way up to the top, so he can launch out and swing down to the ground, and start all over again. It sounds like fun and makes me want to try it.

Mrs. Clancy pauses in her reading, and I look up to make sure I'm not getting the stop-that-doodling look, but she just stares out the window for a second, like she's daydreaming too. Then she starts reading a new part of the poem, and the speaker finally sounds like the old guy in the picture.

"So was I once myself a swinger of birches.
And so I dream of going back to be."

He talks about how hard life is, and then, there's a line that really gets my attention.

> *"I'd like to get away from earth awhile*
> *And then come back to it and begin over."*

I think about those lines again. "I'd like to get away from earth awhile . . ." I wonder where Nonna goes when she slips away from us in her mind.

Is she off swinging birches?

Or out catching leaves?

It seems like she stays away a little longer every time.

Does she like it better there than here?

The bell rings, and I pile up my papers to put them away.

Maybe that's what we need—a bell to bring Nonna back when she's gone off somewhere in her mind. I'd be ringing it all the time.

After lunch, I ace my sixth-period French quiz because Madame Wilder lets us write *or draw* parts of the body as she reads the vocabulary words out loud. I may not be much of a leaf collector, but I can draw everything from my *tête* to my *pieds,* no problem.

But ninth-period science class hangs over me like a big old storm cloud.

I spend the rest of the school day hoping for a homework miracle. Okay, maybe not a miracle. Just a stroke of luck would be nice. Aren't there leaves *anywhere* around this school?

I look on the floor in the hall, just in case someone tracked one in on a shoe. I check the garbage bins, in case some over-achiever like Zig threw out a few extras. I hang out by open windows, hoping a leaf will blow in. I even offer to help the dairy delivery guys carry in the flats of little milk cartons at lunch so I can get outside. The cafeteria monitor says no, and when it's time for ninth-period science, I'm still leafless when I plop down in my seat.

I look around. No one's in class yet except Mary Beth Rotwiller and Bianca Rinaldi, and they're huddled in a corner gossiping about Ruby Kinsella, whose pants ripped when she bent over to pick up the quarter Penny Smith dropped in the lunch line. Apparently, Ruby had on purple day-of-the-week underwear with the day written all around the edges on the elastic. There it was for the world to see: "TUESDAY ** TUES-DAY ** TUESDAY." The fact that it's Monday made it about a million times worse for her. Ruby missed French because she went home to change her pants, and Mary Beth and Bianca are making sure that everyone knows. They are poison sumac trees in the forest of Ethan Allen Middle School.

But at least Bianca's attention is off me.

A breeze ruffles my hair, and I turn to the window. The sunshine must have tricked Mrs. Loring into opening it, even though the air is starting to feel winter-cold.

Lucky for me, there's a garden right outside the window with a crab apple tree dropping bitter little apples all over and an overgrown lilac still holding on to half its leaves. I pick up my pencil and wander over to the sharpener next to the window. I put the pencil in and start grinding its already pointy end to a sharper tip, looking at Mary Beth and Bianca, still huddled and whispering, probably waiting for Ruby to show up so they can laugh in her face.

I leave my pencil in the sharpener and reach out the open window. I wish I had longer arms. The crab apple tree is still about six inches out of my reach. I push the window up a little higher and lean out a little more. Mary Beth and Bianca are now repeating the Ruby story to anyone who will listen.

There's no sign of Mrs. Loring, so I hop up onto the counter next to the pencil sharpener, lean back out the window, and wrap my legs under the counter to hold on. Jackpot! I feel cool leaves in my hand. I grab a few and casually lean into the room to deposit them next to the binder on my desk.

A few more kids have shown up for class, but most of them have joined the Mary Beth and Bianca news hour, so I decide to go for it.

I go back to sharpening my pencil for a minute to make sure the coast is clear. It's reduced to a pointy little nubbin. I hop onto the counter and lean out in the other direction. Unfortunately, the lilac bush isn't quite as close to the building as the crab apple. I have to lean out a little farther, and I can almost touch the closest branch when I hear, "Gianna Zales! What on earth are you doing?"

Mrs. Loring's shrill voice scares me so much I forget to hold on with my legs, and I tip over backward right out the window. I land on my back staring up at the bright October sun, shining through the leaves left on the lilac bush. A breeze stirs the branches, and one drifts down, fluttering off my nose onto the ground. Mrs. Loring leans out, looking first alarmed, then furious.

"Sorry. Just getting some fresh air." I offer a weak smile and sit up to brush myself off. I know I'm in trouble, but strangely, I'm not upset. I'm thankful. Number one—I wasn't wearing a skirt. If I'd gone tumbling out that window with a

skirt on, it would have knocked Ruby Kinsella out of the lime-
light pretty quick. And number two—the custodians must
have just mulched the garden for the winter. I landed in such
a nice deep pile of wood chips that it didn't even hurt. I grab
the lilac leaf that fell, climb in the window, and take my seat,
just as Zig walks in and the bell rings. Mrs. Loring just stares.

"See me after class." She turns on the LCD projector
that's attached to her computer. "Okay, everyone. Take out
your ten leaves so I can come around to check."

Ruby usually sits in front of me. She's always scribbling in
her marble notebook, so sometimes I can sort of hide behind
her when I don't have my homework. She must have decided
she couldn't face Bianca and Mary Beth again because her
seat is still empty.

I raise my hand. Sometimes it's better to get these things
over with quickly, like pulling off a Band-Aid.

"Yes, Gianna?"

"I left my leaves in my dad's car."

Bianca lets out a snort of laughter.

"All of them?"

I nod. "Oh . . . except these." I hold up my lilac and crab
apple leaves from the window.

Mrs. Loring sighs. "You can work on identifying those.
Take out your leaf key and a pencil."

I reach into my pencil bag. It's empty. While Mrs. Loring
walks down the row of desks on her leaf-checking tour, I zip
back to the pencil sharpener, retrieve my nubbin, and settle
down to work.

CHAPTER 6

I escape Mrs. Loring's room after school with a promise to be prepared for the next class and a ten-minute safety lecture. Can't really blame her for that. It's hard to argue after you fall out a window, no matter how low it is to the ground.

Zig's waiting for me outside the school, fiddling with a bunch of wires hooked up to one of those little Christmas-tree lightbulbs.

"Wanna go for another hike?" He clips two wires together and frowns when nothing happens. "Or did you get the rest of your leaves when you fell out the window?"

"How'd you know? You weren't even in class yet when that happened."

"Word travels fast."

I'll say. Ruby never showed up for ninth-period science, but she ought to send me a thank-you note. My tumble into the mulch upstaged her Tuesday panties in a big way.

"I didn't fall, exactly. I sort of tipped over."

"Huh, bad connection." Zig pulls a scrap of aluminum foil from his backpack, tears off a tiny shred, and winds it around the base of the lightbulb. He fiddles with the wires again, and the lightbulb blinks on, Christmas green. He looks up at me and pulls a sliver of red cedar mulch from my hair.

"Hey, don't throw that out!" I grab his wrist. "Don't we get extra credit for bark samples and stuff?"

"Seeds, berries, and fruits. No bark. Peeling it off causes damage. Mrs. Loring says we can't be running all over town killing trees for the sake of an A."

"Fine." I dig into the small pocket of my backpack for the half cookie I saved from lunch. The only thing our cafeteria does right is the molasses cookies. I break the half in half and offer a piece to Zig.

"Are you busy tomorrow? Remember we have the day off for that teacher workshop." He bites into his piece of cookie. "I could help you collect more leaves."

"I don't think I can. I've gotta go shopping with my mom, and Nonna wants to stop by Mrs. Disilvio's house if there's time. Her husband died this morning and she doesn't have many friends here, so Nonna's helping her plan the service. They need to pick out a casket."

"Maybe after school Wednesday then? We could hike again."

"Great."

"Cool, it's a date then."

"A date?"

Zig looks down at his wires. The Christmas light makes his nose look green. He brushes his hair from his eyes. "I mean, not a date. Just a plan. You know, to finish our project." Coach blows the five-minute whistle for practice, and Zig looks relieved. "See you then."

Instead of going inside to get changed for practice, I sit down on the school steps and watch Zig hurry down the street, dry leaves crunching under his maroon high-tops.

Huge maple trees tower over the sidewalk here. Their leaves are almost all bright red now. When school started, they were so green and full of summer. They don't even look like the same trees anymore. I bend down to gather a few leaves and wonder how something I walk past every day can suddenly feel so new.

I dash inside, change into my shorts and T-shirt, and check my watch. 3:28. Two minutes to spare before cross-country practice. I step out into the sunshine, take my warm-up laps, and join the group already stretching at the edge of the track.

"I bet she was too embarrassed to come back." Bianca Rinaldi is bending over to stretch her hamstrings. Her blond hair hangs in shiny curtains around her face.

"I'd stay home, too," says Bianca's sister Jenny, who is a year younger but wearing the exact same shiny purple warm-up suit with matching earrings. "Kevin Richards drew a picture of a girl in purple underwear and put it up on the bulletin board outside the art room! It had a caption that said, 'What day is it today?' " She laughs.

My stomach tightens when I figure out they're talking about Ruby and her ripped pants. She must have decided she wasn't up to facing this crew after she went home to change her pants during lunch.

"I mean, you weren't surprised when they ripped, were you?" Bianca has turned to stretch her right leg, leaning into a new crowd of girls. "She wears the tightest jeans I've ever seen. I swear she's had that faded black pair since fifth grade."

"Ummm . . . I'm pretty sure they were garage-sale material even back then." Jenny takes a swig of her water and pulls her lip gloss from her gym bag to repair the damage from her drink.

"She can't help it that her family doesn't have much money." I say it quietly, but everyone turns as if I've shouted in a church.

"I'm sorry, Gianna." Bianca raises her eyebrows at her sister, and they walk over to me. I should have kept my mouth shut. "You'd know all about garage sales, wouldn't you? I'm pretty sure I saw your *boyfriend* wearing the pants my dad sent to the thrift shop last month."

"They're just so *retro*." Jenny smiles like she's invented a new word.

Bianca high-fives her and joins in. "Gianna knows all about retro. Check out her running clothes." She eyes the *Darn Delicious Dogs* T-shirt Uncle Bob gave me from his drive-in restaurant. Hers says *Princess* across the front. "Of course, it makes sense you'd have a fantastic sense of fashion, with your parents' business and all. Do you get to choose the outfits for the dead old ladies?"

Mary Beth has joined the circle now too, wearing the same warm-up outfit in pink. I stand there, trying to think of something, anything to say, when Coach walks by.

"Let's go, ladies! Get to it!"

Bianca and her clones leave in a cloud of laughter, and I can breathe again. I walk to the building, lean forward and push against it with my hands to stretch my calves. They burn, almost as much as my eyes.

I'd have been fine if I'd kept my mouth shut. Ruby's underwear isn't my problem.

But I start a slow jog to warm up, and my brain starts

churning again. Ruby and I aren't best friends or anything, but she's always been nice to me. She's a willow—she's nice to everybody. She doesn't deserve to be trashed by the sparkle sisters.

I haven't picked up my pace yet, so Ellen catches up with me on my second lap, starting her warm-up run, too.

"Sorry I'm late. I was printing up brochures about these new water bottles." She waves one at me. "I'm going to ask Coach if we can get them for the team so people don't keep blowing through the disposable ones. Want to do a few repeats on the track before we start our route for today?"

"Sure. Which route are we running?"

"Coach's favorite. Behind the school, over the footbridge, and down Mulligan Street to the old water tower. Then up Stetson Ave, back to school." Ellen's falling behind me a little, so I drop back to stay with her.

"Hey." She turns to me and a drop of sweat falls off her nose. Ellen's a dwarf mulberry, like Dad. Only shorter. A dwarf mulberry sapling. I slow down a little so she can keep up.

"Did you hear about Ruby?" she asks when she catches her breath.

Not again. I thought Ellen was different from the poison sumacs. I shake my head a little.

"I don't really want to talk about it." I pick up my pace.

"But I thought you two were kind of friends." Ellen speeds up, and I slow down, confused. I'd been expecting more underwear talk, and given what happened earlier, I can't decide if I want to say I'm her friend or not, even though we've been lab partners a few times. It's not safe to be friends with someone who's Bianca's target of the day.

"You heard about her grandmother?" Ellen asks.

"No." I know Ruby and her mom live with her grand-mother. Once when Ruby and I were waiting for Mrs. Loring to hand out the protozoan samples, we got talking and laughing about how much food you have to shove down when your grandma cooks dinner or risk insulting her if you eat fewer than three servings.

"She died."

I stop running and turn to Ellen. She stops too and nods, her mouth drawn into a grimace. "My mom just told me when she came to drop off my gym bag. It happened right when Ruby was home changing her pants at lunch. Her grandma stood up from the table and started to take her soup bowl to the sink, and she just collapsed. Ruby ran and called nine-one-one while her mom tried CPR. When the ambulance came, the EMT people used those electric shock paddles and every-thing, but it didn't work."

"Wow." I imagine Ruby watching her mother trying to save her grandma's life. Watching her fail. I imagine how I'd feel, losing Nonna. How much I'd miss seeing her in the kitchen after school, smelling her fresh warm cookie smells, hearing her soft voice to even out Mom's crisp, strict one. My throat swells up just thinking about it.

"Come on." Ellen nudges me. We start our run, and I'm glad she's there. It keeps me from getting too deep into my head. We talk about the French quiz and the math homework and Miss Mulcahy, the new computer teacher, and how she can walk around in those pointy high heels all day without falling.

When we finish the run, Ellen heads inside to change,

and I lean against the warm bricks of the building to stretch. I bend down and reach past my sneakers until the gravel scratches my fingertips. I try to think about geometry and leaves and things, but my mind keeps coming back to poor Ruby.

Ruby, who's probably further behind on the leaf project than I am now.

Ruby, who missed the review for the math quiz.

Ruby, who has to deal with her too-small, ripped jeans and her purple Tuesday underwear and Bianca's teasing and Kevin's mean picture on the bulletin board.

Ruby, who doesn't have her grandma anymore to tell her it will be all right.

CHAPTER 7

When I open our front door, the smell of burned sugar stings my nose. The door to the funeral home is closed. Dad must be with a client—a living one, not a dead one—so I leave him alone and head up to the kitchen. A sharp gray haze hangs in the air and makes me cough. How come the smoke detector didn't go off? And where's Nonna? She should be home.

I drop my backpack, run to the oven, and yank open the door. Black smoke pours out in a monster cloud and burns my eyes. When I stop coughing and wave away enough smoke, I can make out a cookie sheet with sixteen charred black lumps. I grab the oven mitt and pull them out so fast that half go skidding off onto the floor. The tray clatters on top of the stove. Even out of the oven, the cookies keep smoking like crazy, so I grab the sheet again, run out the back door, and drop it sizzling onto the damp grass.

I pull off the oven mitt, my hands shaking, and go back inside.

"Mom?" She's usually busy on her laptop when I get home, but she doesn't answer.

"Nonna?" No answer.

I run to the stairs and step on a burned cookie, crushing

it to black crumbs. "Nonna!" I call up, but she's not there either.

Where is everybody? How could the cookies be practically on fire and no one noticed? I need to go get Dad.

I start downstairs, but I hear Nonna's door open, and when I turn around, she's stepping into the kitchen.

"Gianna?" She looks tired, like Robert Frost in that picture, but with longer hair and softer eyes.

"Nonna, what happened?"

She waves the smoke from her face. "I think the cookies might be done."

"Done?" I stare at her. Nonna has probably made three hundred batches of wedding cookies since she moved in with us. They're always perfect. Every single batch. It drives Mom crazy. She's never burned them. Never. Not once.

Until today.

She reaches for the oven mitt.

"Nonna, I already got them out."

"*Grazie*, Gianna. They were done then?"

"*Done*? They were way past done, almost on fire. Can't you see the smoke? Didn't you smell it? How could you not notice?" When Nonna takes a step back, I realize I'm shouting. "Didn't the smoke alarm go off?" I try to keep my voice calm, but it's shaking.

"Well, I heard the loud beeper thing a while ago, but I couldn't figure out what it was. I followed the sound and took out the batteries so it would stop. Then I guess I went in for a little nap." She yawns.

I can't stop staring. She heard the loud beeper thing? And took out the batteries?

Nonna tucks a few strands of white hair behind her ear and smooths her skirt. "It's all right, Gianna. One batch of cookies isn't the end of the world. We'll make more. Okay?" she asks. She waits for me to answer.

I take a deep breath and try to make my voice calm for her. "I turned the oven off, Nonna. Why don't you rest a little more, and I'll help with dinner when the smoke clears out."

"And then tomorrow we'll make more." She pushes my hair away from my face and looks at me. "You'll help?"

I nod. "Sure. I'll help," I hear my voice say. "It's not a big deal."

But it is. Client or no client, I need Dad. As I head downstairs to the mortuary, another burned cookie crunches under my sneaker.

CHAPTER 8

The front door slams shut as I'm walking downstairs, and the door to Dad's prep room is open again so I step inside.

"Gianna?" He raises his eyebrows and looks up at me, still in my track clothes. I usually go right up to change and do homework, so I don't see him until dinner.

"I really need to talk to you." I follow him into the room where he does the embalming. He stops and turns to face me, arms crossed over his chest. There's a body under a sheet on the table behind him. Dad doesn't like anyone in the room when he's working, except Roger, who works for us and helps him sometimes.

"It's important." I cross my arms too. "It's Nonna."

Dad's hands drop to his side like he's deflating. He nods, and right away I can tell that he knows. "I do need to keep working," he says, lifting a makeup case from the shelf, "but you can stay. Talk to me while I work." He folds back the top of the sheet, and I see a chubby-faced woman with white hair, each of her eyes held closed with an eye cap so they don't pop open when her relatives come to see her tomorrow. I can tell she was pretty, even though Dad hasn't put any makeup on her yet.

"I'm not embalming her because the calling hours are happening so soon—tomorrow," he says, opening a jar of moisturizer and dabbing some on her cheeks. It makes it easier for him to put on makeup. "So you don't need to worry about the chemicals."

The embalming chemicals make my eyes sting. The makeup, though, is just like regular makeup, except it's a special kind, made for dead people.

"Find me a darker one of these." Dad holds up a small bottle of foundation.

"I guess you didn't hear the smoke detector go off today." I hand him a jar that's a little darker, but he shakes his head. I look for more. "Nonna was making cookies."

"For Mrs. Kinsella's family?" He nods at the woman on the table.

Mrs. Kinsella. Ruby Kinsella's grandmother. She looks like the kind of woman who was probably baking cookies this morning, too. Things sure can change fast.

"So she burned them?" Dad takes the case from me, since I'm not offering much help. He chooses a darker jar of foundation and rubs some on Mrs. Kinsella's chin.

"She didn't just burn them. She *burned* them. Then she left them in the oven, and when the smoke detector went off, she got mad that it wouldn't stop and took out the batteries."

Dad twists the cap onto the foundation and turns to me. "She took out the batteries?"

"Yes."

"And then got the cookies out of the oven?"

"No."

He sighs. "You found them after school?"

"I walked into this huge smoke cloud, Dad. Worse than the day you started that fire in the fireplace without opening the thing that lets the smoke out the chimney."

"The flue," says Mom. She's been standing in the doorway for a while. I can tell because she has the same serious expression as Dad.

Mom's heels click across the floor as she walks over to the prep table. She picks a dark pink shade of blush from the makeup case. "Try this one."

"It's kind of dark," Dad says.

"Look at the picture." Mom hands Dad a photograph of Ruby standing next to her grandmother at our fifth-grade graduation two years ago. Her grandmother has on as much makeup as a movie star.

"Strawberry bronze shimmer it is," says Dad.

"Gianna, I know Nonna's been acting differently lately. I see it too." Mom starts poking through the lipsticks, taking off the caps and holding them up to the light. "But you have to realize that misplacing things and forgetting things are part of getting older. Just the other day, I left my laptop in the kitchen and looked everywhere before I remembered."

I stare at Mom while she checks out another lipstick shade. Is she kidding? A laptop in the kitchen is a thousand miles from dentures in the apple drawer. And a million miles from ignoring an oven full of cookies practically on fire and turning off the smoke detector. Dad knows. He stops working on Mrs. Kinsella, takes the lipstick from Mom, and puts his arm around her shoulders.

"Angela, you have to admit your mother has been more distant lately. Gianna says she really was lost at the market.

Maybe it's worth a trip to the doctor, just to run some tests and make sure everything's okay. He might even be able to give her something to help."

Mom wiggles away. She's never been very cuddly. She purses her lips. "I think a checkup is always a good idea, so of course, I'll schedule one. But I'm sure it's nothing." She clicks across the room, out the door, and up the stairs, where the kitchen door thumps shut like a period at the end of a sentence.

CHAPTER 9

Tuesdays are always crummy days. They're too close to Monday and nothing good ever happens. There's no school today because of a teacher workshop, but it's still a Tuesday.

When I climb down the ladder from my loft, I step on the to-do list I taped on the ladder last night. Part of Mom's time management lessons. She says I waste too much time. Here's what's on my list:

1. Get up.
2. Brush teeth.
3. Eat Cheerios.
4. Help Nonna make more cookies.
5. Find twelve more leaves.
6. Write "Birches" poetry response journal entry.
7. Run.
8. Shower.
9. Ruby's grandmother's wake.

That last one isn't on my list because I'm likely to forget. I was up half the night thinking about it. It's there because I feel like I need time to get myself ready.

It's weird. I'm in a funeral home all the time. I live upstairs. I go with Nonna to wakes. Heck, I eat wedding cookies with dead people almost every weekend.

But this is different. Ruby will be there with her mom. I know how important her grandmother was to her. I know how important mine is to me, and I can't stop imagining what it will be like to lose her.

Nonna is singing "That's Amore" in the kitchen already, and her mixing bowls and cookie tins are clunking and clanging. Looks like I'm going to have to skip straight to number four.

"Morning." I yawn and shuffle down the stairs. I've pulled on some old jeans, and I'm still wearing the shirt I slept in— an oversize tee from the Metropolitan Museum of Art with a Jackson Pollock painting on the front. Modern art is perfect for baking. No matter how much batter drips on it, no one notices.

"Shall we bake?" Nonna looks a million times better. I can tell she slept well. Her eyes sparkle and her cheeks are pink. She's even wearing a little lipstick. I try not to think of Ruby's grandma and her lipstick downstairs.

Nonna has already sifted the flour, which is fine with me because I can't do it without making a huge mess, and Mom goes crazy when I track flour all over the house on my socks. Ian has plastic baggies over both hands, getting ready to grease the cookie sheets. He's wiggling his loose front tooth with his tongue while he rubs a pat of butter between his hands.

"Hey, Gianna! Wanna hear a riddle?"

"No." I pick up a measuring cup and start packing in butter with a rubber spatula.

"Okay, ready? What did the tooth fairy say when she had to testify in court?"

"I don't know." I pack in some more butter. "What?"

"She promised to tell the tooth, the whole tooth, and nothing but the tooth!"

Nonna laughs. "Clever boy." She kisses him on top of his head.

"So, Gianna . . . you're going to the wake today," Nonna says, turning to me. I can't tell if it's an invitation or an order. She puts a warm hand on my elbow and moves me aside so she can preheat the oven.

"Yeah, I'm going to stop in." I try to sound casual. Maybe it won't feel like such a big deal then. The cup's full, so I scoop out the butter with the spatula. It lands in the bowl with a plop and makes a little poof of flour.

"Cool!" Ian grabs another full stick of butter from the counter and drops it from way overhead so a giant white cloud flies up from the bowl.

"Okay, that's enough help from my big boy." Nonna sends Ian off with another kiss.

"Your friend is going to need you at that wake today." She uses a fork to fish the extra butter out of the mixing bowl. "It's going to be a tough day for her."

"She's not really that close a friend." I start to tell Nonna that I really just know Ruby from science class, but she fixes me with a glare that shuts my mouth before anything else gets out.

"Gianna Zales. Growing up in this house, you've seen enough of life and death to know that everyone needs a friend on a day like Ruby is about to have. You be that friend today. And tomorrow, too."

She stirs the cookie dough more briskly than she really needs to. I've upset her.

Part of me just wants to breeze downstairs later, drop off the cookies, and keep walking right out the front door. But I won't. Because Nonna's right.

I put on a mitt and open the oven door so Nonna can slide in the cookie sheet. A blast of heat hits me in the face and makes my eyes tear up.

When the cookies are safely out of the oven and sprinkled with powdered sugar, my favorite ingredient, Mom comes to help clean up, and I decide it's okay for me to go out to pick up leaves. Nonna hunches over the kitchen sink, scrubbing the mixing bowl and lecturing Mom about a better way to store her bakeware. If Nonna went away from earth a while, like it said in that poem, she sure is back now.

I step outside but need to go back for a sweatshirt. The air has that chilly, damp, going-to-rain-any-minute feel to it. The leaves in the neighbors' yards are whipping around in the wind. I better collect fast.

I dip down to pick up a leaf blowing by, but it's another oak. I shove it in my pocket anyway, along with a sugar maple that scratches across the sidewalk. How come the guy who planned this neighborhood didn't include a better variety of trees? Everybody has a maple and a few little shrubs in the front yard and oaks and cedars in back. I'll never get twenty-five at this rate.

I pause at a crosswalk, and a Green Mountain Leaf Peepers tour bus stops to let me cross the street. A row of people Nonna's age smile down at me from the tinted windows, and a couple wave. I wave back, but I bet they wouldn't be so happy about Vermont leaves if they had to collect, identify, and label every single one they saw.

I wander down the street to the neighborhood with all the big new houses along the river. Maybe they have different trees. Mr. Randolph, our school principal, lives there, and in his backyard, I finally spot a tree that's different from the ones I already have. It's a squatty little thing with funny, fan-shaped leaves. It will be easy to identify since it's so unusual.

I look around. It's too windy for anyone else to be out walking. The fence isn't very tall. It's not the kind of fence you build if you're serious about keeping people out, I decide. In fact, it's the kind of fence you put up to make your yard look pretty and inviting, when you actually don't mind if people come in at all.

But Mr. Randolph isn't exactly a friendly neighbor. He has the meanest face I've ever seen, like he just ate something rotten and can't get it out of his teeth. He's so tall he has to duck down when he walks through the doorway to his office at school, and then he looks all hunched over at his desk. Kids leave that office crying all the time.

Those fan-shaped leaves are calling me, though.

I check the driveway. No cars. And no lights on in the house. I find a foothold and pull myself up to sit on the fence. I perch there for a minute, waiting for the dog. I don't actually know if he has a dog, but it's been my experience that if a vicious dog is going to show up, it shows up when you're trapped somewhere, like inside a fence you've just jumped. There's no barking, so I drop to the other side.

It's the coolest backyard I've ever seen, and not just

because of the funky fan-leafed tree. Exotic-looking shrubs decorate all the corners, and some bright fuchsia flowers are still blooming next to the pumpkin vines along the fence, even though we've had three nights of frost.

I grab a few leaves from the short tree—it's nice to be able to reach them, for once—and then notice another tree whose leaves I don't have yet. This one towers over the yard—a Mr. Randolph tree. It has feathery leaves with a whole bunch on each stem. I think Mrs. Loring's leaf key calls it a compound leaf. Whatever it is, it would look great in my collection.

There's just one problem. The lowest branch is at least eight feet off the ground. On my very tallest day, I'm five four. I look around to see if there's anything I can stand on. There's a little rocking chair out on the patio. It's not very big, but it would probably give me enough of a boost that I could grab onto the branch and pull myself up.

I jog over, pick up the rocking chair, and settle it under the lowest part of the tree. Carefully, I step up and wait to catch my balance. I can't quite reach, but I decide it's jumpable. I bend my knees, shaking when the chair wobbles, and spring up into the air.

I grab onto the branch and dig my fingertips into the scratchy bark on top. My body is sort of swaying back and forth from my jump, and my sneakers are dangling above the seat of the rocking chair. It occurs to me that jumping back onto a rocking chair will be a lot harder than jumping off it. Why do I always think of these things too late?

Well I'm here now, so I might as well get the leaves. Except the leaves are way out at the end of this branch, swaying in the wind.

I'm clinging to the middle of the branch, also swaying in the wind.

I decide my best bet is to imagine I'm on the monkey bars, so I dig my fingernails deeper into the bark, force myself to let go with my left hand, and move it in front of my right hand. I'm swaying like crazy, and the bark is digging into my palms. But I manage to scoot forward a few more times. The branch gets skinnier out at the end, so it actually gets easier to hold on. I'm within one scoot of the leaves when I hear a soft crackling and then—

Crack!

The branch snaps off in the middle, I tumble to the ground in a heap, and it bounces off my shoulder into my lap. I rub my barky hands together and do a quick check for injuries.

My ankle is a little sore from landing on it wrong, but otherwise, I'm okay. And I got the leaves—a whole branchful.

Then the sliding glass door in the back of the house slides open.

Mr. Randolph is standing there in a gray Navy sweatshirt and baby blue flannel pajama bottoms, which doesn't sound scary, but it is. He has the look he gets on his face right before he screams at kids in the lunchroom. I wonder if I can be expelled for this, since it's not actually at school. I decide not to ask.

"Miss Zales." He slides the door shut behind him and folds his arms. His feet are bare and he has enormous toes. They're tapping the deck planks while he talks. "Somehow, you seem to have wandered into my yard."

"Yes, sir."

"Somehow, you failed to notice the fence that encircles my yard." Tap, tap.

"Yes, sir."

"Yes, you failed to notice it?" His eyes get huge, and I know yes is the wrong answer.

"No, sir. I, er, climbed over it to get a leaf for my leaf collection." I look down at the four-foot branch I'm still holding and lift it up a little. "For science class."

He makes a noise that's a cross between a laugh, a snort, and a growl and comes down the back steps toward me. He stops at the base of the big tree, looks down at his rocking chair, and moves it aside. "Do you know what kind of tree this is?"

"Not yet, no." I consider explaining about the dichotomous key that we're using but decide it won't help.

"Have you noticed, Miss Zales, that nothing is growing around this particular tree?"

I hadn't. But he's right. The other trees all have little hills of flowers around the bottom. Not this one.

"Do you know, Miss Zales, why nothing is growing here?"

I shake my head.

"I will tell you, Miss Zales. It's because this tree is a black walnut. A black walnut looks quite attractive, like any other tree. It has lovely foliage." He looks at the branch in my hand. "But you already knew that, of course."

I nod. I wish he would just call the police and have me arrested.

"But the black walnut is deceiving. It looks perfectly attractive, like a fine addition to a garden. But all the while, it releases a toxin into the soil that kills off other plants; it poisons anything growing nearby.

"A black walnut, Miss Zales, is like the student who fails to show respect. He—or *she*—might look like a good person. But underneath, at the roots, he—or *she*—is spreading the poison of disrespect." He turns and climbs back up his steps to the glass door. "You'll leave my yard now." He points to the other corner of the house. "By the gate."

I nod but don't say anything. I'm out of "yes, sirs." I consider dragging the black walnut branch along with me, but he's still standing on his porch, so I leave it and shuffle toward the gate.

Black walnut.

I am *so* not a black walnut.

He's the black walnut on this block.

The glass porch door slides open, then closes with a thump, and I stop, still ten feet from the gate.

I don't even check to see if he's watching. I dash back and yank a handful of leaves off the branch, then run for the gate again.

These will be easy to identify later.

I know a black walnut when I see one.

CHAPTER 10

Sbrigati, Gianna! Let's go!" Nonna calls from downstairs.

"I'm hurrying," I say.

But I'm not.

I stand by the window, buttoning Mom's maroon sweater, looking out at clouds as dark as the black dress she loaned me for the funeral. What am I going to say when I see Ruby?

"I am so sorry for your loss."

"I'm so sorry about your grandmother."

"I'm sorry you lost your grandmother."

That last one sounds like she misplaced her grandmother in the garage or something. Nothing sounds right.

Nonna always does the talking. I carry the cookies. She always seems to know just the right thing to say.

"I'll think of her every time I hear wind chimes," she told Mr. Caprici last month. His wife had the noisiest porch in the neighborhood. She made her own chimes out of sea glass she found on their trips to Cape Cod.

"Her memory will live on in your garden," she told Mr. LeBelle, whose wife grew roses in ten different shades. And here's my favorite:

"He died doing what he loved best," she told Mr. Salsbury's

wife. He was killed when a rogue salmon pulled him overboard during a fishing trip in Alaska. Nonna always knows what to say. Not me.

"Ready, *bambolina*?" Nonna's in her funeral wear, her black jersey dress with the charcoal wool sweater. I think there are still cookie crumbs in it from last weekend.

"I guess so." I collect my bushy hair into a fat barrette and look in the mirror. Red hair looks so undignified, like you've worn the wrong clothes to a formal event.

"The important thing is that you talk to her." I swear Nonna reads my mind. She knows I have no clue what to say. "Tell her you're sorry, yes, but then just sit with her and chat."

"Chat? About what? Her grandmother's going to be right there in the casket. How can she chat?"

"Gianna, it's almost noon." Nonna points to the clock. Calling hours started an hour ago. "By the time we get downstairs, Ruby probably will have been hugged by at least thirty strangers saying how sorry they are about her grandmother. You can say that, too. But you're her friend. Talk to her about school and what's for lunch in the cafeteria and your leaf project—things from *her* world. The grown-ups who work with her mom can't give her that kind of comfort today."

But I can. I think about that and follow Nonna downstairs. She hands me the tray of cookies, arranged on a thick white doily. Nonna opens the door, and I step in, ready to join the end of the line of people paying respects.

Except there is no line. There's just Ruby's mom, who looks like Ruby with shorter hair and more wrinkles around her eyes, standing by the casket. There's a woman who might be her mom's sister. Her eyes are clear green, like Ruby's, and she's talking quietly with Mrs. Kinsella near the casket. I almost don't see Ruby at first. She's over in the corner with her marble notebook tucked under her arm, flipping through the guest book. She's as far from the casket as she could possibly be. A little boy with messy black hair is playing with a dump truck at her feet, making "vroom" noises. Ruby looks down and puts her finger to her lips to shush him.

"Cindy, I'm Francesca DiCarlo. Your mother sat behind me in church, and she always sang with the most wonderful energy." Nonna has managed to set down the cookies, uncover them, and take Mrs. Kinsella's hand in one fluid gesture.

I look over at Ruby. She squats down, her long limbs all folded up, and moves the dump truck back and forth with the kid, but she's staring at the casket.

"My granddaughter Gianna and your daughter are good friends at school," Nonna says, grabbing back my attention. Ruby's mom looks at me, probably wondering why she's never heard my name if we're such good friends. Then she nods.

"Ruby has mentioned you, Gianna. You were lab partners last year, right? She said you let her borrow your notes after she was absent."

"Um . . . yeah." Ruby had missed two days of class. I'd just pushed my notes over to her when class started, so she could copy them to catch up. It didn't seem like a big enough deal to talk about at home, especially since my notes aren't the greatest.

"Oh, here's another girl from school, I think." Mrs. Kinsella looks up. Ellen steps through with her mom, who must have come right from the hospital where she works. She's wearing white instead of black but doesn't seem worried about it. She walks right up to Mrs. Kinsella and hugs her, while Ellen wanders over to me.

"You girls will want to talk." Nonna gives us a little push toward Ruby and dump truck boy. He's probably about three and reminds me of Ian at that age, full of snot and too much energy. Not quite a tree—just a shrub. The kind that looks all shaggy and bright red in the fall.

"Hi, Ruby," I say. She turns to me and opens her mouth to say something, but the kid beats her to it.

"My name is Warren Washington Kinsella Junior." He wipes his nose on his hand before offering it to me. I shake it and wipe it on Mom's sweater.

"It's a pleasure to meet you, Warren Washington Kinsella."

"Junior," he corrects. Ruby rolls her eyes, but Ellen and I laugh.

"Can I write in that?" Warren Washington Kinsella Junior tugs at the corner of Ruby's notebook.

"No. But you can color. Here." Ruby pulls a couple of crayons out of her pocket, tears a page from the back of the guest book, and sends Warren Washington Kinsella Junior off to draw.

"Not like we're exactly filling up those guest book pages anyway." She watches him leave. "Might as well use them."

"I thought there would be more people." I look around. "I mean, usually . . ."

"I guess other people have big families that come and hang around." Ruby flips to the front of the guest book. "The ladies in Grandma's Red Hat Society came right at eleven because they had a potluck lunch scheduled for eleven thirty and didn't want to miss it. Mom's friends from work came early too, on their lunch break. And you guys," she adds. "Thanks."

"I'm really sorry about your grandma," Ellen says, and she gives Ruby's shoulder a little squeeze.

"Me too," I say.

Ruby just stands, picking at the corner of the guest book.

"You missed the French quiz. You can borrow my notes if you want," I say, and immediately wish the words were attached to me on a string so I could reel them back in. Like she cares about a French quiz right now.

"Thanks," she says quietly.

And then I don't know what to say until I hear the big oak door open again. "Here comes somebody else." Maybe they'll know what to say.

Two blond ladies come clicking in on their high heels. One is a little taller, but otherwise, they could be twins. They're both wearing suits with short skirts.

"Hmph." Ruby's mouth turns up, but it's not a smile. "That's my mom's boss with her assistant. Does she look familiar?"

I stare at the blue eyes and model blond haircut. It does look familiar. Subtract about twenty years, and you'd have . . .

"Bianca?"

Ruby nods. "It's her mom. Michelle Rinaldi. Watch. You'll see more family resemblance."

"Kinda hard to miss," Ellen whispers. There's a bottle of fancy spring water sticking out of Mrs. Rinaldi's bag. That alone would be enough to make an enemy of Ellen.

But there's more. The taller woman sashays up to Ruby's mother and takes her hand, but not the way Nonna held it. She holds it more like you'd hold something you pulled out of the drain in the kitchen sink. Her mouth is tight and her words are clipped while she talks to Ruby's mom. She nods curtly and struts away with her assistant tagging along behind her, never looking toward the casket once. She is mistletoe, I decide. Pretty and poisonous. Like Bianca. As Nonna would say, the apple doesn't fall far from the tree.

"Well," I say. "I guess we know where Bianca gets it."

Ruby nods. "The day my pants ripped must have been the greatest day of her life. I heard she went around telling people like it was the most important news in the universe."

"She's a jerk, Ruby," Ellen says. "You're worth twenty of Bianca."

"Thanks."

"See my picture?" Warren Washington runs back up to us waving a colored guest book page. "It's Ruby, and she's smiling because she's the bestest person I know."

Ellen bends down to get a closer look. Ruby looks over at her mom, talking with Ellen's mother. And I think about Ruby. I think about how quiet I was when Bianca and Mary Beth were laughing at her, and my face burns. I wonder how Ruby would feel if she knew I didn't stick up for her much.

Nonna walks over. "Would you girls like to come say a prayer with me?"

"Sure," I say. Ellen nods. Ruby shakes her head and starts flipping through the guest book again.

I follow Nonna, kneel next to her, and scoot over to make room for Ellen. We say a Hail Mary and an Our Father, and Nonna talks quietly into the casket. She tells Ruby's grandmother what a beautiful family she has and how nice her voice sounded at church last week, as if Mrs. Kinsella might sit up and say, "Thank you." When she's done, Ellen and I both make the sign of the cross and walk back to Ruby, who's hunched over, writing.

"Is that a journal?" I ask her.

"It's just stuff I write. Poems and stuff." I want to ask more, but her hair falls over her eyes like a curtain over a window and she doesn't look back at me. She reaches the end of a line in the notebook and twirls her pencil in her fingers.

"I guess you've already spent a lot of time at the casket, huh?" Ellen says.

Ruby looks up from her notebook with shiny eyes and shakes her head.

"I can't," she says, looking down and flipping through the pages. They're almost all full. "I keep remembering her at lunch yesterday, standing up with her bowl and then dropping it and falling on the floor. It was so loud and awful. I see it over and over in my head. Mom on top of her doing CPR and those rescue guys with the shock paddles." She closes her notebook. "I don't want to see any more."

I take her hand because that's what Nonna always does, and I think about the woman I just saw, laid out in the casket. There's nothing chaotic or scary about her. She's wearing her blue-and-white daisy dress with her gold hoop earrings. Her eyes are closed, and her face is relaxed and peaceful. Her cheeks are rosy, and it doesn't look like strawberry bronze shimmer blush. It looks like she had a good life, and she's off somewhere, dreaming about it now.

And then I know what to say.

"Ruby, your grandma wouldn't want you to remember yesterday morning. That's not what she was all about." She sniffles and nods, so I keep going. "You and your mom are hurting right now, but she's not. She's someplace else—someplace good and quiet and peaceful. You should—I mean—I think you need to—I think it might help you to see her now."

"I don't know." She bends down to pick up Warren's dump truck and spins the front wheels.

"My dad made her look really pretty, just like in the picture at our fifth-grade graduation."

"You saw that?" Ruby looks up at me. I nod. "That was one of my favorite days with her ever. She told me how proud she was, and we went for chocolate chip ice cream at Nelligan's Dairy."

"She'd be proud of you today too," Ellen says quietly.

Ruby glances over at the casket, puts down her notebook, and takes a deep breath. "Will you come with me?"

I take one of Ruby's hands. Ellen takes the other, and we walk to the casket. At first, Ruby just stares at her grandmother in the big oak box, and I think I might have made a mistake. But then she kneels down. I start to kneel too, but she puts up her hand. Ellen and I step back.

Across the room, Ellen's mom says something that makes Ruby's mom laugh a little. Nonna offers Mrs. Kinsella a cookie. She takes it.

Behind me, I hear Ruby's voice.

"Hi, Grandma . . . It's me."

CHAPTER 11

Mom's waiting at the counter with her purse over her shoulder when Nonna and I come back upstairs with our empty cookie plate.

"Where have you been?"

"We were downstairs," I start to explain.

"I know where you were."

Then why did she ask? I start to argue, but Nonna pokes a pointy, eighty-three-year-old elbow into my ribs, so I shut up. Mom sighs.

"I told you we were going to go to Crafty Cats to get supplies for your leaf project this afternoon. I only have an hour now because I need to be back to help Dad wrap things up downstairs, and we can't go tomorrow because I have a Junior League meeting, so after school, you and Dad need to run Nonna to the doctor for her *checkup*." She emphasizes the word "checkup," daring us to suggest it's anything else.

"Tomorrow already?" Nonna puts down the cookie platter. Ian swoops into the room and licks his finger to pick up the crumbs left on the plate.

"Yes, well, he had a cancellation and I figured the sooner the better." Mom fishes car keys out of her purse. "Let's go."

"Just let me change." I pull my arms out of her sweater and drape it over the railing on my way upstairs. Two minutes later, I'm in jeans and my Picasso T-shirt. It's a little wrinkled from being scrunched up on my closet floor, but it's still clean. Mom frowns at it.

"Why can't you wear something where the people's noses are in the right place?"

I look at Nonna for help. She raises her eyebrows and looks up at the ceiling. I grab my backpack and follow Mom and Ian to the car.

"Hold this, please. I'll tell jokes on the way." Ian hands me *The Giant Book of Riddles* while he gets buckled in. Ian is a spiny cocklebur plant—the kind with the seeds that grab you with those sharp little barbs and never give up. Thank God it's only a ten-minute ride.

"Now," Mom says, twisting around to look behind her as she backs out of the driveway, "I found your leaf collection planning worksheet in the Garbage Pit when I was picking up your room. You got glue all over it so it was stuck to your math quiz."

"Did you sign the math quiz?"

"No. Why would I sign the math quiz?"

"I was supposed to have you sign it last week."

"What did the boy ghost say to the girl ghost?" Ian starts laughing before I can guess.

"I don't know, what?"

"You're BOO-tiful."

"I'll sign it when we get home. It's stacked on your desk now with your other school papers. I threw out those shredded-up magazines."

"You threw out my collage stuff?"

"And what is all that paint splattered on the wall?"

"What wall?"

"The wall behind the mountain of stuffed animals."

"Oh . . . they were sort of supposed to stay there."

"Gianna, you need to take some responsibility. Life isn't a big joke."

"Okay, here's one," Ian says. "Why can't you go hungry at the beach?"

"Ian, please." Mom flips on her turn signal. "Gianna, that leaf collection planning worksheet—you've read it, right?"

"Because of all the sand which is there!" Ian laughs hysterically.

"I think I read it."

"Get it? All the sand which is there?"

"Ian, please." He closes his book and looks out the window.

"I collected leaves this morning," I offer.

"How many?"

"Four more. I'm up to seventeen now."

"How many brave guys named Ian does it take to change a lightbulb?" Ian asks.

"I don't know, one?"

"Gianna, we're having a conversation about your leaf project here. You're way behind."

"I have leaves. I just need to find a few more and get them all together."

"Nope, that's not the answer. Guess again." Ian ignores Mom's warning look in the mirror and reaches across the backseat to poke my arm. "Come on, Gee. How many brave guys named Ian does it take to change a lightbulb?"

"Ian, please."

"None! Because brave guys like me aren't afraid of the dark!"

I groan.

"Enough!" Mom's glare is about to burn a hole in the rearview mirror.

"I made that one up, you know," Ian says quietly, and opens his book again.

"So, Gianna, you know you need to have twenty-five leaves for Thursday?"

"Yes."

"And you know they all have to be different kinds?"

"Yeah. Mom, for once, I'm on track with this. Let it go, would you?"

"And you know they all have to be identified with annotated note cards, sources, and information about geographic distribution of the species?"

Say what?

The shell-shocked look on my face tells Mom-in-the-mirror two things. One: I didn't know that, thanks very much. And two: the leaves are not identified, much less annotated or notated or any other kind of tated. I always miss the fine print.

"Gianna." She sighs and zips into a parking spot close to the door of Crafty Cats. "You really need to get yourself organized. It's so easy to make lists and keep things sorted out."

Easy for you, I think as the automatic doors slide open. The potpourri section is right by the door, so coming in here is like walking into a giant flower garden. Mom's eyes are watering. She hates it, but I love it. I bought a big bag of potpourri once and used all the dried petals and buds to make a mosaic of a little girl in a garden. Nonna has it on her closet door because it makes her clothes smell good.

I stop to smell a bag of potpourri and have to run to catch Mom, who has taken a cart, loaded Ian into it so he won't grab everything, and hustled past needlepoint and embroidery by the time I catch up. She pauses next to the scrapbooking aisle.

"This may have what we need."

What "we" need turns out to be a sturdy binder with acid-free paper, plastic sleeves to protect the acid-free paper, little stickers to decorate the pages, index cards for labeling, and an assortment of cut-out leaves and tree stencils for decorating the cover. Mom's excited.

"It's going to look so neat and polished!" She grabs another pack of leaf stickers for good measure. Ian snatches some Star Wars stickers and slips them into the cart while she's not looking.

We hustle past bags of Halloween cobwebs, Thanksgiving turkey decorations, and in the next aisle, artificial Christmas trees waiting for their turn in the front of the store.

I want to check out the good paintbrushes because I'd love to get a fan brush for my acrylics, but Mom keeps looking at her watch, so I don't bother asking. I help her unload the cart. The cashier scans our binder and stickers and sleeves, beeping and beeping, and filling the bags. I laugh, remembering what Mrs. Loring said about the leaf project when she first assigned it.

"This doesn't need to be a fancy or expensive project. Leaves, after all, are free!"

The last set of leaf stickers goes through, and the register beeps out a grand total.

Here's a riddle for you. How much does a free leaf project cost when Mom decides to take charge?

Forty-eight dollars and nineteen cents.

CHAPTER 12

Now that I'm well supplied, I might as well get started.

I toss the Crafty Cats bag onto my desk and start picking up sweatshirts and wind pants off my bedroom floor so I can find my bag of leaves. It was under here somewhere.

Except it's not.

I move Miranda and the other animals to a new corner, in case they were all ganged up, sitting on my leaves. They weren't.

"Hey, Nonna?" I call.

"What is it?" she hollers up from the kitchen.

"Have you seen my bag of leaves?"

"What?"

"Have you seen my bag of leaves?" I shout.

"Your gasoline?"

"Bag of leaves!"

"Oh." Long pause. "I think there are some in the living room."

The living room? I don't remember putting them there, but okay. Nonna pads up the stairs in her slippers.

"Here you go." She drops an armload of *Good House-keepings* on my desk. Magazines.

No bag of leaves.

"Thanks, Nonna." I don't have the heart to tell her it's the wrong thing, so I tuck them into a drawer for a collage later on, and I head downstairs.

"Mom?"

"Mmm?" She doesn't look up from her Sudoku. Dad's leaning over her shoulder, pointing to one of her little number boxes.

"Have you seen a bag of leaves around?" I ask.

"No!"

"You haven't?"

"The nine can't go there! There's already a nine in this column, and I can't move it because of this four." She looks up at me. "What did you say?"

I might as well move on to Dad. "Have you seen my bag of leaves?"

"Leaves?"

Is there something strange about the way I say "leaves"?

"Yes, leaves."

"Were they in a ShopRite bag?"

"Yes!" Finally, a spark of light.

"One of the medium-sized plastic ones?"

"Yes, where are they?"

"Well, we found them in the back of the hearse when we were unloading Mr. Disilvio." He looks up from his paper. "They were moldy, and I figured they were just extras. Did you need them?"

"Yes, I need them! Where *are* they?"

"I threw them in the garbage."

I run out to the garage in my socks, pull the garbage bag

out of the can, and tear it open. I yank out two empty cereal boxes, a bunch of funeral home junk mail, casket brochures and ads for hearse replacement parts, cucumber and carrot peels, toss it all behind me, and paw through what's left in the bag.

No leaf bag.

Tears sting my eyes. That bag has to be here. It *has* to.

I turn the bag upside down and shake it. Coffee grounds splatter on the cement floor, and something soaking wet lands on my foot. It's a wad of paper towels drenched with the orange juice that Ian spilled this morning.

Where are my leaves? I shake the bag again harder. Please let me find them. Let them be stuck to the bottom or something. Just let them be here.

With one last shake, an empty bag of potato chips, stuffed way in the bottom, flutters to the floor.

That's it.

No leaves.

I tip up the garbage can and look all the way into the bottom. Empty except for a few stupid flies.

There have to be more trash bags somewhere. I start moving bikes around, trip over my kickstand, and stumble into the metal shelves where Dad keeps his garden tools. The edge rips my shirt and scratches my shoulder so it bleeds, and the tears finally spill down my cheeks.

Dad pokes his head out the door. "Gianna?"

"Where *is* it? Where's the garbage from this morning?" The lump in my throat is so tight I can barely find breath to speak, but I do. "I *need* those leaves."

He takes a deep breath. "Gianna, that's what I came to tell you. I'm pretty sure that garbage got picked up this morning."

He nods down at the pile of vegetable peels and shredded credit card offers at my feet. "That's all from today. I'm so, so sorry." Dad walks over and reaches to put his arm around me, but I pull away.

"Those were all of my leaves. All of them! What am I going to *do*?" I bend down to start picking up the garbage so he won't see me crying harder.

He bends down and starts scooping up coffee grounds with the edge of a cereal box. "Were they all in that one bag?"

I nod. "Except for a few I got this morning."

"Where are those?"

I think. "In the pocket of my jacket."

"Can you start with those, at least?"

"I could, I guess. But it's not going to matter. I'm never going to finish now."

"Go on, Gee. You can start, and we'll figure something out. I'll clean this up." He scoops up the soggy orange juice towels.

I stub my toe on the edge of the door on my way inside, and the sobs rise up in my throat all over again. This time I can't hold them back.

I slam the door, plop down on the hallway floor, rub my toe, and cry.

My socks are all black from the garage floor. I've gone from having almost twenty leaves to having just the four I picked up this morning, and I'm not even positive where those are. They're probably moldy too.

Finally, I catch my breath. I take my puffy face and red eyes up to my room, reach for my running jacket, and unzip the pocket. One of the leaves—the oak, I think—has gotten all crumbly, and I can't really tell its shape anymore, but the others are okay.

I'm never going to get this done now. No chance.

I don't know why I'm even bothering, but I pull out the fiery sugar maple, the one I know for sure. I take a deep, shaky breath and label it on an index card. I start flipping through the book. I'm supposed to sketch a map of where the tree grows. I'll need colored pencils for that, so I find the new ones I bought two weeks ago with Nonna. It's an amazing pack, with every cool color you can imagine. Not just basic reds and blues, but shades like scarlet tangerine and smoky indigo. Perfect autumn sky colors. Looking at them doesn't make any more leaves appear, but it makes me feel a little better.

I flop the leaf book upside down to keep my place and hold the maple leaf by its stem, twirling it around under my light. It's an incredible mix of colors. There's the usual red, but also yellows and browns and leftover green and even little hints of shady purple. I wonder if it's possible to make those colors if you're not a tree.

I pull out scarlet tangerine and rub the pencil across a blank piece of paper, making the rough shape of a maple leaf. I choose lemon lime for the edges near the stem and shade just a little bit of deep forest near the middle. It takes half an hour, but when I finish, I've used seventeen different colors to come up with a leaf that almost matches the one in my hand. It's worth keeping, so I sign it—

Gianna Z.

I open the leaf book and find an oak leaf to sketch, since my real one is in little brown crumbles that I've blown off the desk to the floor.

"Gianna! What are you thinking?" I didn't even hear the door open. Stealth-Mom is staring at the colored pencils as if she just walked in on me running an organized crime ring out of my room. "Dad told me about your leaves. Why on earth aren't you at least getting started with what you have?"

I slam my honey-nut brown pencil onto my desk. "Because all of my leaves are in yesterday's garbage except for these." I hold up the pile, and more oak bits crumble to the floor. "That's why." My eyes burn, but I blink fast. With Mom, tears always make things worse. I swallow. "And then I thought I'd draw some of the leaves I had because . . . you know . . ." When I say it out loud, it even sounds dumb to me.

A tear gets out.

Mom darts out of the room and is back in two seconds with a handful of Kleenex. "Wipe your face and get your shoes on. I'm taking you out to collect leaf specimens."

"What?" It's after four o'clock. "Aren't we going to eat soon?"

Nonna steps into the doorway. "Where's the salad dressing, Angela?"

"In the fridge, Mom, where it always is." She takes a deep breath and lets it out in a big huff. "And leave it there for now. Gianna has work to do on her leaf project."

I catch Nonna's eye while Mom unpacks the Crafty Cat bags and starts lining up plastic sleeves and stickers on my desk. Nonna shrugs her shoulders, just the tiniest bit. She knows Mom better than anyone, well enough to know when there's no stopping her.

"But I'm getting hungry," I say.

"I'll pack you a snack," Nonna says, and turns to Mom. "Where are you going to take her?"

"I have no idea, frankly, but she needs to get moving on this project. Do you realize she's had almost a month to do this? A month, and here we are . . ."

"Let's walk the Frost Trail," Nonna says quietly, and pulls Mom toward my door. "We haven't been there in ages. I'll come too."

"You're not really in any shape for a hike, Mom."

"Hike, schmike. It's paved most of the way. I'll be fine. And I like reading the poems along the trail."

"Nonna, I really don't want to go on a hike. I'll just go out around the block."

"Nope." Nonna picks up my sneakers from the floor and pushes them into my chest. "Get your shoes on. Your mother's right."

Mom walks out the door and nods, happy to be right and have someone tell her so.

At least she's done nagging for now. But Nonna's supposed to be on my side. Always. How could she have turned on me like this? I plop down on the floor to put my shoes on.

"Pssst!" She pokes her head into the doorway again. "You'll be better off on the Frost Trail. They label the trees with little markers so you won't have to identify them later." She disappears but comes right back. "Don't tell your mother."

I finish lacing my shoes. "Don't worry. I won't."

CHAPTER 13

The Frost Trail is only six miles outside of town, but we never come here anymore, now that Ian and I are old enough to climb real mountains. This one's more of a nature path, really.

"Here." Mom hands me a shoe box full of plastic zipper bags and markers. She pulls my leaf identification key out of her purse. "You're going to do it right this time. Identify and label them as soon as you find them, and then seal them in the bags, and you can put them into the binders neatly when we get home."

Somehow, this trail was more fun when I was little and my zipper bags were full of graham crackers instead.

"Come here, Gianna." Nonna points to a big wooden sign at the trailhead:

Robert Frost lived and worked within a mile of here. The fields and forests were inspirations for his poems and are mentioned in many. A leisurely half-hour walk will acquaint you with Frost country and some of his works that are located in appropriate settings. To enjoy this trail, please take your time and leave nothing but foot-prints.

"Let's *go*." Mom squeezes past us. "There are a lot more trees once we get in a little ways. Hurry up. It's almost five. It's going to start getting dark soon, and we still need to fix dinner for the boys."

We left Dad and Ian playing Star Wars LEGO Attack. Dad kept watching to see when Mom left. I bet he's already brought out the hidden potato chips. Somehow, he and Nonna both deal with Mom better than I do. We're just so different.

I watch her power-walking along the boardwalk. I stay back with Nonna. Mom doesn't stop to read the first poem posted along the trail, but Nonna does.

"Read it out loud, okay?" I ask, and she leans in to read the neatly typed verse, posted at the edge of a marshy clearing.

It's called "The Pasture," and it reads like an invitation. A guy going out to rake leaves from the spring in the pasture invites somebody to come with him. Maybe it's his wife or his son. "You come, too," he says, like there's no hurry at all.

"I bet that guy doesn't have a leaf collection due on Friday," I say.

"No, I'd imagine not." Nonna squints off into the woods as Mom disappears.

"Look, another one right here." I set my shoe box and leaf key down on a weathered wooden bench and step to the railing at the edge of the marsh. I had to stretch up on my tiptoes to see over the top last time we were here. I was only six or seven, but I remember the electric blue dragonfly hovering over the swamp grass. Everything was so green and bushy then. It must have been July or August.

Now the plants are all brownish and rustly dry, like they're whispering secrets. The poem posted there is called "The Secret Sits." It's about how we humans have to go around guessing at everything while the world keeps its secrets.

"What's that supposed to mean? I don't get it."

"That's what it means," Nonna says laughing. "That there are things in this world we just don't get."

Nonna walks on down the boardwalk, but I stay and look out at the whispery marsh again. I try listening harder. Maybe the tall grasses know Nonna's secrets about getting away from earth. I wish they'd tell me how to keep her here.

"Gianna!" Mom's hiking boots clunk on the far end of the boardwalk, so I jog ahead to meet her.

"Where are your leaves?" she asks.

"I haven't got any yet. We were just reading the poems."

"Where's the box?"

"Oh. Back there." I whirl around to run and get it from the bench, but I don't go quickly enough to miss hearing her sigh.

When I catch up, we cross a wooden bridge that looks like it ought to have trolls under it and then walk up a steeper part of the path into shadowy trees.

"Are you doing okay?" Mom asks, and she slows down to wait for Nonna.

"I'm fine, Angela. I hiked this trail with you in my arms plenty of times. I think I can hike it now."

"Could you still do it carrying Mom?" I ask, and even Mom laughs.

She helps me identify a gray birch, a red spruce, and a hemlock, and labels them with neat block letters in permanent marker on the plastic bags. During breaks, Nonna reads us poems: "The Road Not Taken," "Going for Water," and "Stopping by Woods on a Snowy Evening."

"That's the only one that doesn't fit," I say.

"How so?" Nonna asks.

"Well, the place, I mean. The poem about the road less traveled is right where a trail splits off. The one about mowing is in a low area with lots of tall grass. The one about going for water's at the edge of the stream. But this one," I gesture toward the mess of bushes and weeds and pine trees behind the "Stopping by Woods on a Snowy Evening" plaque, and I shake my head. "All this has nothing to do with the poem."

"Not today, maybe," Nonna says. "But imagine this spot in another season when the pine boughs are drooping with snow."

I squint at all the green. "Maybe," I say. "But it's hard."

"It is hard," Nonna says. "But you're an artist. You should know there's more to a story than the part happening right now."

"Here." Mom hands me another couple of leaves. "They're from this tree right behind you. Use your leaf key to identify them. I'm going to try and find us a spot to rest that's out of the wind." She zips her jacket and walks ahead.

"Or you could just use that," Nonna whispers and points to the sign at the base of the tree. I write "beaked hazelnut" on another plastic bag and zip the leaves inside.

When Nonna and I catch up to Mom, she's brushed all

the dead leaves off a long wooden bench, sheltered on three sides by big old trees.

"Get a few leaves and join us," Mom says pointing up at a branch that still has leaves hanging on.

"I have this one." I pluck a leaf and hand it to her. "It's a white oak. I'm going to go on ahead, okay?"

"That's fine," Mom says. "We'll be along soon."

I flip through the plastic bags in my shoe box while I walk, and I have to admit Nonna's idea was awesome. I have eighteen leaves from this walk alone, added to the four I think I still have at home.

I round a bend in the trail, and the trees thin out until there are just low bushes on each side. Blueberry bushes, I think, but it's too late in the season for berries. I watch for sweet spots of dark blue anyway, walking with my head down until I trip and go sprawling into damp leaves and bang my elbow on a root so hard I have to catch my breath.

I hold on to my box of leaves though. For once.

And then I look up and have to catch my breath all over again because the killer root belongs to the most incredibly fantastic climbing tree in the entire universe.

I know climbing trees. Zig and I have climbed every tree in our neighborhood that's even the tiniest bit climbable. Even Mr. Webster's crab apple, and that one's really hard because he doesn't cut it back enough, so there are skinny branches sticking out all over the place.

But this one. This is the great-grandmother of all climbing trees.

Robert Frost must have been a climber. I bet he grew this

tree special for climbing and had somebody cut it back every year so it would have perfect branches for footholds. They're perfectly spaced. They're the perfect thickness. Just far enough apart but not too far. Perfect.

And the best part is that the branches go all the way to the top without turning into the skinny ones that might snap under your feet. They stay thick and sturdy.

This is no climb-halfway-up-and-run-out-of-good-branches tree. It's an all-the-way-to-the-top tree.

I balance my leaf box on the root that tripped me. For a second, I think about stopping to identify this tree, but it's way more fun to climb it.

So I climb instead.

Without having to stop or find a new route even once, I'm within a Gianna-length of the very top—probably forty feet off the ground, at least.

And my perfect tree has a perfect view. The shoe box on the root looks tiny from up here. But the mountains, all hazy purple in the distance, still look big and old. And the trees are amazing. My eyes skim the tops of fluffy red and yellow trees still holding on to September, then swoop down into the dark spaces where the leaves have already fallen, where black branches scratch the edges of the hills.

Mom and Nonna wind their way toward the clearing until they're almost right underneath me, but they don't spot the shoe box, tucked just off the trail, and I don't make a sound.

Their voices drift up into my branches.

"They'll be getting hungry. I'll call and have him preheat the oven."

"Or I can do it when we get back. Relax, Angela. Enjoy the sunshine."

The path through the forest was already darkening with tree shadows, but here in the clearing, the last rays of late afternoon sun make it feel a lot warmer.

"It is a pretty nice day." Mom tips her head up to the sky. I duck behind a branch so she doesn't see me. "Fall still makes me think of Dad," she says.

"It was his favorite." Nonna's voice is quiet as they take the turn in the trail that heads back to the parking lot, and I strain to listen. I've never heard much about Mom's father because he died right before I was born. "Remember how he'd take you out picking apples in the orchard and hold you way, way up to get the ones on the highest branches?"

"I always thought they looked sweeter," Mom says.

She laughs, and as I watch her reach out to help Nonna step over a tree that's fallen across the trail, it's a little easier to imagine a Mom other than the list-making, tofu-eating, three-ring-binder-organizing Mom of right now.

I climb down, jump the last five feet to the ground, pick up my shoe box, and run to catch up with them.

"Well, there she is," Nonna says. "Our leaf catcher. We thought you'd gone up ahead."

"I did, but then I found a great climbing tree," I say. "It had perfect branches. They were just the right—"

Mom frowns at me, licks her finger, and smudges it against my cheek. "You have pine sap on your face."

But Nonna reaches for Mom's hand and pulls her back. "Let her be, Angela. The tops of trees are always sweeter. You know that."

Mom looks over at me. "Sappy girl," she says, but she smiles a little and lets my face stay dirty all the way to the car.

CHAPTER 14

"Please stand for the Pledge to the Flag."

I stand, but I pull my backpack up onto my desk so I can look for my English papers while I'm pledging allegiance. I never got to do my homework last night because we got back so late and then dinner was late and then Ian tried starting the dishwasher with laundry soap inside and the kitchen got all wet and bubbly. After we cleaned it up, I had to go to bed.

I pull my crumpled poetry response sheet from my backpack. For some reason, it smells like applesauce. I reach in my bag for a pencil and feel something mushy. It's the apple I brought for a snack after cross-country. Bruised, juicy, and mushy. I toss it into the garbage near my desk and read the journal question:

What might Robert Frost mean when he writes, "One could do worse than be a swinger of birches"? Write your personal response in a paragraph.

This is the very worst kind of assignment. When teachers ask for a personal response, they never mean it. They want a school-acceptable personal response, which kids make up based on what we're pretty sure they want us to think. It's not what we really think, though. I toy with the idea of writing the real deal this time:

I think Robert Frost is saying that a little daydreaming and playing isn't such a bad thing at all and that teachers ought to lay off when a kid gets caught looking out the window. We're not plotting to make bombs or something; we're just taking a little time out from a boring lecture to think about important stuff like the school dance or what's for lunch. I really hope it's pizza. Robert Frost probably would have failed English at this school because he'd be looking out the window instead of writing these responses all the time.

And if he had written the responses, he would have failed science, too, because he would have written poems about birches instead of collecting their stupid leaves and pasting them into an overpriced binder with index-card labels. And then someone like Bianca probably would have made fun of his poems when he was done.

I am done writing now and will be looking out the window for the remainder of the period.

What I really write is this:

I believe that Robert Frost writes, "One could do worse than be a swinger of birches" to show readers the value of imagination. I'm an artist, so I know that painting can take you away from earth a while, just like his

trees took him into the clouds. But Frost also says in the
poem that we need to come back to earth and get things
done. He probably had to go milk cows or something,
and we all have to pay attention and do our work.

Gianna Z.

When I turn in the response in English, I double-check to
make sure it's the second one—not the real deal—that I hand
to Mrs. Clancy.

All day long, I double-check my backpack to make sure my
leaves are there for science, and for once, I don't lose a single one.

On my way to science, I check one more time. I have the
four from my run this weekend, plus eighteen more from my
hike, and most of those are already labeled in their bags, so
all I have to do is make up the index cards. I can get three
more by tomorrow, easy.

Mrs. Loring has the field guides and identification keys
laid out on our lab tables, so I know it's going to be a workday.
Perfect. I pull up a chair next to Zig and Ruby, who are table
partners. I'm surprised she's back in school already. She looks
tired and sad, like part of her is still there at the funeral home
with her grandmother. But she has a pile of leaves in front of
her that she somehow managed to collect in the middle of it
all. A few more are sticking out of her marble notebook like
bookmarks.

Zig has his leaves pressed inside a giant phone book that
definitely came from a city bigger than ours. Our town's

phone book is about as thick as my pinkie finger. I look at the cover.

"Rochester, New York?"

"My dad left it that time he visited four years ago. He spent our whole camping weekend on his cell phone, making business calls." Zig runs his hand over the phone book cover and looks a little sad. I hate that, so I blurt out something stupid.

"What kind of tree is your dad?"

He looks at me for a second, then looks down at the phone book.

"The kind that doesn't grow around here."

Ruby reaches for the phone book, flips it open to the restaurant section of the yellow pages and pulls out a perfectly flattened leaf the size of my face.

"What's that one?" she asks.

"American chestnut. I couldn't believe I found it." He holds it up and smiles at it the way parents smile at a newborn. "They're really rare now, you know?" I didn't know. But I'm not surprised that Zig found it. He must have at least forty leaves, almost all of them numbered and linked to corresponding note cards with facts already.

"Gianna?" Mrs. Loring has appeared behind me in one of those stealthy moves only moms and teachers are capable of. I hate that. Teachers should have to wear cowbells. She raises her eyebrows at my backpack. "Do you have your leaves? Let's make good use of this work session."

"Yes, Mrs. Loring." I open my folder to show her, but my colored-pencil leaf drawings are on top. I move them so she can see I have real ones, too.

"Nice job. It looks like you're all caught up." She hands me a field guide, and by the time the bell rings, I've identified all but a few of my leaves.

"I'll see you after practice?" Zig waves, and I nod. "Bring your stuff. We can work on the project at my house."

I grab my books from my locker and open the door to a perfect running day.

Coach jogs over with her clipboard and falls in step with me during our warm-up lap.

"Science project coming along, Gianna?" She has an asterisk next to my name on her roster.

"It's coming along great," I say, and I feel Bianca's eyes burning into the side of my face. She'd been running with Mary Beth on the inside of the track, but as soon as Coach started talking to me, she weaseled her way over and edged into the lane next to ours, tipping her head over to listen.

That's just fine. I'll give her something to listen to.

"My project is just about done," I say loudly, and for once, it's the truth. "I just need three more leaves."

"Good, good . . . glad to hear it. I'm counting on you, you know. Sectionals are a week from Saturday."

"I'll be there."

Coach jogs away, and I can't help smiling over at Bianca, who looks even nastier than her usual poison sumac self.

Today's workout is a trail run on the winding path through the woods behind school, so I warm up with a lap on the track. Then I take off into the trees at full speed, breathing in big gulps of autumn. Fallen leaves have their own unique smell, an awesome earthy smell you don't get when you're running on pavement. Your feet have to be crunching the leaves into the dirt, over the rocks, and then you can smell it all around you.

I'm not even a little bit tired when I come out the trail on the other side of the woods, sprint down the street, and take the last turn around the block to head back to school. My four miles go by too fast today, so I take a few extra laps on the track. I meant to pick up my last three leaves along the way, but I always zone out when I run. I'll get them on the way home.

With my extra laps, I'm the last one out. I could run forever today, but it's getting late, so I take a long drink of water and head inside to get my stuff.

The locker room is quiet, but what I see when I come around the divider hits me like an explosion.

Papers cover the floor. Papers with English poetry responses. Papers with fractions converted to decimals. Papers with my name on top.

My stomach clenches, and I feel like I'm going to throw up the water I just drank.

What happened?

I pull open the locker where I put my stuff before practice. Nobody ever locks their lockers. You're not supposed to have to lock anything in Vermont, not even your front door. But the hook where I hung my jacket and the shelf where I tossed my backpack an hour ago are empty.

My leaf project was in that backpack.

I slam the locker shut and start opening the other ones, up and down the row of benches.

Nothing.

I drop to my knees and start rifling through the papers on

the floor. The leaves have to be here somewhere. They have to be.

The little floor tiles dig into my knees. I shuffle every last paper into a pile and don't find a single leaf.

Through wet eyes, I see a blur of red over at the sinks. My jacket's balled up in one of the basins, soaking wet. Who would do this? As soon as the question forms in my head, I know.

Under a bench, I find my science binder, empty. She ripped the papers right off the rings, so I can't even clip them back in. I fling the binder against the row of lockers, and the clang echoes off the yellow tile walls of the shower room.

When I look up, there's my backpack. Flung into a shower stall, damp from sitting under the dripping faucet. All around it are empty plastic bags. Note cards that used to be matched up with leaves for my project sit in soggy puddles, with ink running off in little streams across the tiles. The leaves are scattered everywhere—like a storm blew in the window. It blew in an empty water bottle, too.

My eyes burn. I press the heels of my hands against them—hard. I'm not going to cry. She wins if I cry. And that's not going to happen. Not now.

But I feel like I can't breathe in here anymore. I open the door to the hall and head for the drinking fountain. Bianca and Mary Beth are heading down the hall from the front entrance with Coach Napper. Bianca's carrying the first-aid bag and looking up at Coach like she's the president.

If I look at her, I'm going to lose it, so I stop in front of the drinking fountain. But my teeth are clenched so tight I couldn't take a drink if I tried.

They walk right up to me and stop.

"Shouldn't you be home working on your leaf project?" Bianca says.

The back of my throat starts to close, and my eyes sting again. But I'm not going to do it. I swallow hard and force myself to smile at her.

"I'm not worried about the leaf project—it's just about done." I stare her down. "In fact, I just need to finish picking up a few of my things that got scattered in the locker room. Then I'm heading home to finish. And then I'll probably take a late run after dinner. To get ready for sectionals."

Bianca's smile fades, but Coach doesn't notice. She pats me on the shoulder, says, "Well done," and heads off to her office, with Mary Beth following her. Bianca glares at me for a second and then turns to catch up to them.

I go back to the locker room and shuffle the rest of the papers and bags and cards and leaves into a big pile.

The leaves are okay, even if they're a little wet. They're just not identified anymore.

So I'll do what I told Bianca I was going to do. I'll go home. I'll lay them all out in my room. I'll get out my identification key and start over.

I have to. Because mean, glittery girls do not belong at sectionals.

I'll just start all over again. From the beginning.

Way down the hall, I hear the school's back door slam. Finally.

I sit down on the bench next to my leaves and cry.

When I finally stuff everything into my backpack and leave school, it's almost four.

But Zig's waiting for me just outside the gym door. He had electronics club after school, and he's playing with a doorbell buzzer hooked up to a nine-volt battery. Every time a kid walks out the door, he makes it buzz. It's loud enough so they all turn and look into the building, thinking they've set off some kind of alarm at the door. I set down my backpack, sit down next to him on the warm concrete steps, and take a long drink of water from my bottle.

"How was practice?" he says.

"Good," I say. That's all. If I tell him what happened I'll cry, and that's not an option. Not now. I swallow the lump in my throat and take another slug of water to wash it down.

"Wanna go finish the leaf project?" I don't answer. Zig buzzes an especially long buzz. "It's . . . uh . . . due Friday." He looks at me with that little worried wrinkle between his eyebrows, and it makes me smile a little, in spite of everything.

"I know."

Sometimes he's as bad as Mom. I love him, though. I mean, I like him. Like a good friend. He nudges my arm. My stomach does a loopy flip, and I feel a weird little zip of electricity. He catches me looking at him and brushes his hair from his eyes. I look away and take another drink of water. What *is* it with us lately?

"Gee?" He nudges again, and I jump. Water spills down my chin, onto my shirt.

"What?"

"Sorry . . . should we go get started? I know how much you want to go to sectionals, and I know how you feel about the whole Bianca thing."

"Ha. You don't know the half of it," I say. "I'll finish. I will. I need to get three more and then identify everything."

"Want some help?"

"I always want help." I take a deep breath and reach down to pick up my backpack. "It must be nice to be a genius."

"It has its benefits." One of the freshmen track stars struts by, a tall, lanky kid named Robbie. He pretends not to notice the lowly seventh graders. Zig buzzes him, and he jumps about a mile. Zig smiles, and a leaf flutters down from the tree above us. I reach for it but miss. Zig swoops down and catches it just before it hits the ground.

"Trembling aspen." He hands it to me, and I tuck it into my bag.

CHAPTER 15

When we get home, Dad is helping Nonna into the van.

"Let's go, Gianna." He taps his watch.

Nonna's appointment. I forgot I was supposed to hurry home after practice. I can't work on my project today.

"Can I call you later, when we get back?" I talk over my shoulder to Zig while I reach for the car door.

"You can call me anytime." It sounds like some cheesy line from a movie. I turn around to make a face at him, but he's already jogging away. It must have just come out wrong.

"Sorry I'm late." I toss my backpack into the car and hop in. "Where's Ian?"

"He went home with a friend after school. How's the leaf project?" Dad eyes me in the rearview mirror.

"Good," I lie. "It's just about done." I'm getting good at that one. There's a bag of apples on the floor that Dad must have missed when he unloaded groceries. I polish one on my shirt and take a bite.

"Just about?" We're at a stoplight, so I get Dad's full mirror attention.

"Well, not quite," I admit through my mouthful of apple. I swallow. "I have a bunch to identify. Zig says he'll help me later."

"I think there are some nice trees around Dr. Hebert's office." Dad looks at Nonna, waiting for her to chime in, but she's staring out the window while the old brick buildings of downtown flash by.

"Aren't there, Mom?" Dad puts a hand on her arm, and she jumps, like she had forgotten she wasn't alone.

"Aren't there what?"

"Aren't there lots of nice trees around Dr. Hebert's office? I was just telling Gee that she might get some more leaves there."

"I suppose there might be, yes." Nonna looks out the window. She's quiet today. Normally, she'd be asking me all about my day at school and if I sat next to any cute boys in lunch.

She seems more like herself when we pull into the parking lot, though. She pulls a lipstick from her purse and flips down the windshield visor to open the mirror.

"Have to look my best," she says. "Dr. Hebert is quite a gentleman." She puts the cap back on her lipstick, smacks her lips, and turns to face me. "He once told me I'm his favorite patient."

I grab my damp backpack and follow her up to the office door. "He says that to all the old ladies, Nonna." She laughs her laugh that sounds like a waterfall. I roll my eyes, but I'm happy she's back for right now.

Dr. Hebert must have the coolest waiting room in town. There are giant spider plants hanging from the ceiling and framed modern art prints covering the walls. I see a few Picassos and plan to point them out to Mom when she shows up after her Junior League awards reception to meet us. There's a cool totem pole painting that I'm pretty sure is by a

Canadian artist named Emily Carr. I'm about to check it out when Dad's cell phone starts playing Barry Manilow's "Copacabana."

"You have got to change that to a respectable ring," I hiss at him as he flips it open. Nonna reaches for a *Good Housekeeping* on the table, and I pick up a copy of *People*. That fifteen-year-old movie star Brenda Belinda is on the cover. How come her freckles look cute and mine just look splotchy?

"Okay, I'll be right there," Dad says into his phone. He flips it shut and turns to Nonna. "Mom, I'm going to have to leave to make a home pickup. Angela should be here from her Junior League meeting in just a few minutes. She'll go in with you and talk with the doctor. Gianna can wait with you until then." Dad looks at me and I nod.

Whenever someone dies at home, he needs to go to the house to move the person's body. He has to go right away or they'll call someone else. So he goes. And we understand. It's part of the unwritten rules for funeral home families. When Dad gets a call for a pickup, it takes priority over family dinners and birthday parties. And doctor's appointments, too, it turns out.

"We'll be just fine." Nonna pats my knee and leans over to look at what I'm reading. I hear a *"Tsk."* Must be she noticed Brenda Belinda's skirt, which is about two inches long.

Nonna's doctor is running late, which is good, since Mom seems to be running late too. I've breezed through four weeks' worth of *People,* and Nonna has surreptitiously ripped five recipes out of Dr. Hebert's *Good Housekeeping* and stuffed them into her purse, when the nurse pops her head into the waiting room.

"Mrs. DiCarlo? The doctor will see you now, okay?"

Nonna looks up and frowns. We both look over at the office door. Where's Mom?

"Mrs. DiCarlo?" the nurse says again, and Nonna stands up. I stand too.

"I'll go with you." I expect Nonna to say no and tell me to wait, but instead, she puts a hand on my back and follows me through the door.

"Just hop up on the table, and the doctor will be with you soon, okay?" The nurse is wearing a skirt that's only a little longer than Brenda Belinda's, and she's using an extra-chipper voice that makes me want to give her a good push.

"Well, I don't hop much anymore, but I'll certainly make a go of it." Nonna reaches for the paper robe on the chair.

"You can leave your dress on, okay?" Nurse Brenda chirps. "Doctor Hebert will just be asking you some questions today, and you'll come back for blood work next week. So just hop on up there, okay?" She pats the table and leaves before I can process what she said. Just asking questions? That doesn't sound like any physical I've ever had. And no, really, none of this is okay.

Nonna looks at the table. "You want to help me out with this hopping?" I pull over a small stool, and she uses it to climb up. "Thank you," she says. "Really. Thank you."

"You're welcome." I'm not sure what we're talking about.

"This may be a rough appointment," she says, biting her bottom lip and swinging her feet a little.

"I'm sure I've seen worse. Remember that time I fell out of Zig's fort and split my knee open on the tree trunk? I had to get seven stitches."

"I remember," she says. She was the one who took me in

to the emergency room. Mom was at a charity board meeting. "But that's not what I mean, really. Gianna, you know I've been having a tough time lately. I can't always come up with the words I want to use when I talk, and—"

"And you lose things," I interrupt. "But you've always done that. So do I."

"It's different." She stares at me, and I nod. I know. I can tell she knows too. It *is* different. And it's getting worse.

There's a knock on the door, but before either of us can answer, Dr. Hebert barrels into the room. "Hello, Francesca! How's my favorite patient?"

Nonna smiles my way. The words "told you so" are written all over her grin.

"Just fine, mostly."

"You look well." So does Dr. Hebert. I see why Nonna put on lipstick. He has black-and-gray hair, all thick and wavy, and bright blue eyes that squint when he smiles. He's a silver maple, I decide. He flips open the manila folder in his hand and pulls a pen from behind his ear as he sits down next to Nonna. Then he notices me.

"Well, hello there! You must be Gianna, the artistic and beautiful granddaughter." I blush and reach out to shake his hand, hoping that mine isn't too sweaty. I sit down on the other rolling chair next to the table and pull my math book from my backpack so I can get a little work done while I wait for Mom.

"Francesca, Angela tells me you've been having some trouble." I look at Nonna, expecting her to deny it, but she doesn't. She nods.

"She says it's not serious, but she did describe some

issues that concern me. So let's just have a little chat, shall we, and see how things are ticking." Dr. Hebert flips over a page on his clipboard, and his voice takes on a more businesslike tone.

"I'm going to ask you some questions and give you some problems to solve. Please try to answer as best you can."

I still have my math homework out, but I can't look away from Nonna and Dr. Hebert. Her medical exam is going to be an *exam*. And she looks just as nervous as I felt on the day of my French quiz.

"What month is this?" Dr. Hebert holds his pen over the paper and looks up at Nonna.

"October," she says, and I let out a breath. It's going to be easy stuff. She can relax. I go back to my equations, half listening as he asks her about the season, the year, and the day of the week. He names three objects—ball, car, man—and asks Nonna to repeat them and then remember them. She repeats the three things. Nonna's doing great. Maybe she was just tired last week, with the smoke alarm and eggplant incidents. She said she's been having trouble sleeping, so it's understandable she'd be a little more scattered on those days. I'm just about to finish my second problem when it gets very quiet.

"Francesca?" Dr. Hebert raises his eyebrows at Nonna. "Do you know what floor of the building we're on?"

Nonna shakes her head. That's dumb. Of course she knows what floor we're on. The fifth floor. She pushed the elevator button herself.

"But, Nonna . . ." Dr. Hebert holds up a hand to silence me. I frown at my math book. He ought to just give her a minute to think.

"Spell the word 'world,'" he says, and Nonna spells it. *See?* She knows.

"Now spell it backward, please."

There's another long pause. I look at Nonna, and she's squinting at the empty white door of the examination room, as if there are letters there that she can't quite make out. Finally, she shakes her head. He makes a mark on his paper.

"What are the three objects that I asked you to remember before?" Nonna's quiet again. Again, she looks hard at the door. The words aren't there.

Come on, Nonna.

Ball, car, man.

Ball, car, man.

I stare at her and think the words as hard as I can so she'll remember, but it doesn't work.

"I don't know."

"Okay." Dr. Hebert makes another mark on his paper. He should have given her more time or given her a hint or something. That was a while ago, and they talked about other things in between. I can't see how this is proving anything.

Next, Dr. Know-It-All holds up his hand and points to his shiny gold Rolex. "What is this called?"

"It's a clock," Nonna says. Dr. Hebert makes yet another mark on his paper.

"She got that one right!" I drop my math book to the floor and lean over to point at his clipboard. "She got that one!"

"Gianna, please . . . I'd be happy to talk with you about this screening later, but right now, we need to finish."

I was wrong. Dr. Hebert is no silver maple. He's more like a hawthorn, those nasty, two-faced trees I just read about in my leaf guide. They look just great until you go to get a leaf and then you get stabbed with a big, pointy thorn.

I sit down on the rolling chair and push off, away toward the window. I look out. Where is Mom? She'd never let this go on so long.

Dr. Hebert holds up a pencil. "What is this called?"

"A pencil." Nonna breathes out a long breath, like all this is tiring her out. At least she got credit for that one. I'm surprised he didn't mark her down because she didn't say it was a yellow number-two pencil. I pick up my own pencil and start a drawing on the back of my science paper. I try to sketch St. Mary's Church across the street, one of the oldest buildings in town. It has cool arches, and I try to get the lines and shadows just right. It helps a little, but not so much that I can ignore the longer and longer silences that follow Dr. Hebert's questions. Finally, he puts down the clipboard and folds his hands in front of him.

"Francesca, I'd like to talk with Angela about your results, I think. If she's on her way, then perhaps—"

"I don't know where Angela is, and I'm quite able to talk with my own doctor, thank you." Nonna's voice is quiet, but firm.

Doctor Hebert looks at me. "Yes, well, perhaps Gianna should—"

"She can stay." Nonna folds her arms and fixes Dr. Hebert with a look.

"Very well, then." He flips a page on his clipboard. "Francesca, you scored eighteen points on the Standardized Mini-Mental State Examination. That's out of thirty."

"That's pretty good," I say from the window. Dr. Hebert

frowns at me, so I go back to outlining shingles on the church roof.

"There are thirty possible points, and anything over twenty-six is considered normal for a senior citizen. Scores between eighteen and twenty-six show mild but significant cognitive impairment, and anything below that suggests a moderate to severe loss of ability to reason."

Nonna is still looking at him, confused. Like she's not here right now.

I put down my books and scoot my chair over between them. "What does 'significant cognitive impairment' mean?"

This time, Dr. Hebert doesn't frown, but he still looks serious. "What it means is that for whatever reason, it's getting much harder for your grandmother to think and remember, to do the things that have always been easy for her. She's going to need your help at home."

"She's already my big helper." Nonna's back. She takes a deep breath and reaches out for my hand.

I pull it back and point at Dr. Hebert's clipboard. "Fine. I'll help at home. But you haven't said what all this proves—your little checklist here. Why does it matter that she can't remember three words you made up?"

"It's an indicator, Gianna. That's something that—"

"I know what an indicator is!" I feel Nonna's hand on mine again. "I know what an indicator is," I say in a quieter voice. "An indicator of what? What is it and what can you do to help her? Isn't that why we're here?" I try to keep my voice down, but it's hard.

"Yes and no," Dr. Hebert says. How does someone get through medical school and get to be a doctor when he can't choose one answer for a stupid yes or no question? He holds up his checklist. "This test helps us to figure out the extent of your grandmother's problem. But it may be a long time before we know what's causing the changes in her brain. We might never know exactly. But what we do know is that she's going to need some extra help."

"Gianna, Dr. Hebert isn't telling you anything new." Her eyes are shiny with tears. She's right.

"So what happens now?"

"The next step is for us to go ahead with some blood work, which I think we already have scheduled for . . ." Dr. Hebert flips through his papers.

"Next week." Nonna pulls her flowered calendar book from her purse. "The fifteenth." She puts her book away and elbows me in the ribs. "See? Remembered that one."

Dr. Hebert smiles. "I'm going to be honest with you both. This is tough on families. You're probably in for some difficult times. Humor helps. And I know you have a good dose of that in your house." He winks at Nonna and puts a hand on her shoulder. "You're going to have a lot of questions about how to handle things, and your daughter will want to talk with me as well. I know you've probably thought about the possibility of Alzheimer's disease?"

Nonna takes a deep breath and nods. "I have a living will already, and my papers are all in order."

"A living will?" I turn to Nonna. "You have a living will?"

She nods. "It's a document that explains what my wishes are in case I'm not—"

"I know what it is." There was an old guy who had one on an episode of *Critical Care*. His family kept arguing over whether to take him off life support or not, and they ended up having to follow the orders in his living will but they fought about it the whole hour. "How long have you had a living will?"

Nonna takes a deep breath. "Your mother helped me get it together a few months ago."

Now I can't stop the tears. "Mom knows too? And it was *months* ago? How come nobody told me?"

"Because you should be creating your art and running through the mud and catching leaves," she says.

"Well I'm not, am I? I'm here in this stupid office listening to him ask you stupid questions, and my leaf project isn't done, and Mom is off at some meeting with a bunch of ladies while we talk about what happens when you . . ." I can't say the word. I can't. I start sobbing just thinking about what it will be like to lose Nonna.

"I'm not going anywhere just yet." She gets off the examination table and bends down to hug me. "I'm sorry. I'm so sorry you had to go through this with me today." She holds me for a long time.

Finally, Dr. Hebert clears his throat. I'd forgotten he was here. "Uh . . . I think we should probably talk more when Angela is available. For now, you can call if you think of any questions, and otherwise, we'll see you for that blood work next week." Dr. Hebert holds the door open for us. Neither of us talks as we walk through the spider plants and paintings in the waiting room to the elevator. Nonna pushes the button marked *G* for Ground, and I wonder if she's figured out yet which floor we were on. When we step out, Mom is rushing down the hall toward us, teetering dangerously on her high heels and dripping petals from the mini carnation corsage on her gray suit.

"I am so sorry to be running late, but the Junior League gave me the fund-raiser of the season award and the press was there for pictures, so I had to stay, and then that nice Bobby Costanza from the paper wanted to do an interview and I thought it would be great publicity for the funeral home, so I . . ." She looks past us at the empty hallway. "Where's Dad?"

"Pickup," I say. Nonna and I walk past Mom and out the sliding glass doors. We both need some fresh air.

CHAPTER 16

Even Ian senses trouble. When we pick him up at his friend Finn's house, he looks from me to Mom to Nonna, then looks down and plays with his jacket zipper the whole way home while Mom talks about her big meeting.

"Rebecca Gardner had on the prettiest long purple dress. You'd think that would make her look like a big grape, but it really was lovely." She forces a laugh—too high-pitched and too long.

Nonna looks out the window.

I stare at the back of Mom's head.

Ian stares at his zipper.

Two blocks from home, Mom finally asks about Nonna's appointment.

"Well," Nonna takes a deep breath. "The test showed what he called . . . let's see . . ." She looks at me for help.

"He said it showed significant impairment of Nonna's thinking," I tell Mom.

"Sounds like a fancy doctor phrase for getting a little forgetful." She reaches down to turn up the radio.

I raise my voice. "Mom, it's more than that. It's too early to say for sure, but Nonna's still going in to have more tests on the fifteenth."

"So, more blood work next week, Mom, but in the mean-time, everything's A-okay?" She looks at Nonna for a second and then switches the radio station again. I want to scream at her, but I don't say anything. I'm so angry I'm afraid of what will come out if I open my mouth at all.

Garth Brooks starts singing "Friends in Low Places" and Mom taps her fingers on the steering wheel until Nonna turns off the radio.

"Angela, let's talk at dinner. I'm a little tired out."

At home, Mom goes straight to the kitchen and puts on a pot of water for the spaghetti.

"Let's see, pasta's nice and quick. We all need our carbs! Whole wheat, of course. Gotta have that fiber!" She whips Nonna's sauce from last night out of the fridge and puts that on the stove, too. She unloads the dishwasher so fast I'm afraid she's going to break the coffee mugs. The whole time, she's humming a song I don't recognize. I'm not sure it's even a real song.

Dad finally comes up from his office and just stares. Mom whips dinner plates onto the table like those dealers you see on the TV poker games. I'm amazed they don't go flying across onto the floor.

Nonna pulls Dad aside and talks to him quietly. They stand in the doorway between the kitchen and the dining area, watching Mom rip apart a head of iceberg lettuce. He whispers something to Nonna, and she nods.

Mom drops the lettuce on the floor. "Angela . . . Can I do anything to help?" Dad asks.

"Nope, all set. Dinner, Gianna!" Mom yells even though

I'm about five feet away from her. She scoops up what's left of the lettuce, thrusts the salad tongs into the bowl, and heads for the table. Dad flattens himself against the wall to get out of her way.

By the time I finish washing my hands and sit down, Mom has dished up my pasta, smothered it in sauce, and sprinkled cheese on top the way I like it.

"Thanks." I help myself to some salad and pass it to Dad.

"You need your energy." Mom smiles brightly. "Especially with all the schoolwork you have to do. Somebody needs to finish up a leaf collection." She wags a finger at me.

Is she kidding? I spent the afternoon in a doctor's office listening to Nonna flunk her test, question after hideous question, while Mom schmoozed with the Junior League ladies and took notes on their outfits. And she wants to talk about leaves?

"I was supposed to go with Zig today, but I had to . . ."

"That's not an excuse." The fun voice is gone. "You've had weeks to work on this, and it looks like you've spent all your time coloring." She flings a hand toward the counter, where I see my leaf pictures, the color experiments with my pencils, in a messy stack.

"Those are just—I was just looking at the colors. And I have leaves! At least I had some before they got thrown out. I can't believe you're doing this now! You haven't even asked about the doctor. Why are you harassing me?"

"Just because we have some family issues going on this week doesn't mean you can drop everything."

I slam my fork down on the table. "You sure didn't drop everything," I say. "You didn't drop *anything* in *your* schedule today."

"That was an important meeting, Gianna. I'm sorry I was a bit late, but—"

"A *bit* late? You call meeting us in the parking lot after the appointment's completely over a *bit* late?"

Mom picks up her fork and starts moving cucumbers around her plate. "I'm sorry about that," she says quietly. "I really thought Dad would be there." She takes a deep breath. "And I guess part of me didn't want to hear what Dr. Hebert was going to say."

"Yeah, well, neither did I."

Mom nods. "You shouldn't have had to."

Dad puts his arm around her. She lets him. "This is tough, Angela. You're human."

Mom picks a piece of wilted lettuce out of her salad, wraps it up in her napkin, and turns to me. "I know you had schoolwork to do today too. I'll help you tomorrow, okay?"

"I'm fine." I don't want her help.

"I'll help Gianna with her leaves," Nonna says. "Goodness knows she went above and beyond the call of duty for me today."

Mom turns to Nonna. "I'm sorry. I got caught up in things at the luncheon and lost track of time. I should have been at your appointment, I know. It's just . . ."

"I know." Nonna reaches over and pats Mom's hand. Mom looks down at her plate, but not before I see her eyes fill up with tears. Nonna doesn't let her off the hook, though. "Angie, you would have gotten caught up in a trash collectors' convention today to avoid that appointment. I know you see what's going on with me. It's hard to miss. And I know what it's like to watch someone slip away from you. We both do."

She means Grandpa. Nonna's told me before how she and Mom both stayed by his side when he had cancer.

Mom nods and takes a deep breath. "Would you tell me more about today? I'll listen. What did Doctor Hebert say?"

"He gave me a test to measure my thinking and reasoning, and I had trouble with it." Nonna looks over at me and smiles a little. "In spite of Gianna's valiant efforts to get me a few extra points."

I look down and poke at my spaghetti with my fork.

The questions were stupid. The whole thing made me mad. And not just at the doctor. Part of me was angry at Nonna, too, for not being able to answer the questions, for not being able to think the way she used to, and for going away from us.

"Is it Alzheimer's disease?" Mom asks quietly.

"He doesn't know yet. They're going to run the blood tests next week, and even then, it's hard to tell for sure. . . ."

"But?" Mom leans forward and looks right at Nonna.

"But I have a feeling that it is," Nonna says. She doesn't look scared, just tired.

I'm scared, though. I saw a TV commercial once about a walk to raise money for Alzheimer's disease research. It talked about how awful Alzheimer's disease is for families. How it starts with forgetfulness and gets worse and worse. How it affects 4 million Americans.

And now Nonna might be one of them.

CHAPTER 17

The doorbell rings while I'm drying the spaghetti-sauce pot.

"Go ahead," Dad says. "I'll finish." He sent Mom upstairs to rest after dinner.

I open the door. It's Zig with a ShopRite bag full of leaves. "How many more do you need?"

"Two."

"Here." He hands me two leaves taped to labeled index cards. "Black cherry and slippery elm."

"Why is it slippery? Did your leaves get all moldy too?"

He points to the index card. "It's a kind of elm."

"I know." I grin. "Have I ever told you you're my hero?"

"Maybe once or twice. Ready to work?" He raises his eyebrows and I nod, brushing a tangled lock of hair behind my ear. My hair and I have already had a long day.

"Just let me get my binder and we can go into the den," I say. He starts to follow me upstairs to the kitchen, but I hold up a hand. "I'll be there in a sec."

Ca-chick! The cell-phone camera click announces Ian's arrival in the hallway.

"Hey, Zig! Knock-knock . . ."

"Who's there?" Zig always plays along.

"Ummm . . ." Ian's eyes dart around the room. Some-times, his mouth gets ahead of his brain. Finally, he looks down at Zig's bag of leaves.

"Leaf."

"Leaf?"

"That's who's there," Ian says. "Leaf."

"Okay, leaf who?"

"Leaf us alone and knock on somebody else's door!" Ian doubles over laughing as I brush past him to get my leaf binder.

"Be right back," I tell Zig.

Nonna's teakettle is boiling on the stove when I walk by. I worry for a second, but she gets it right away and pours her-self a cup. It's only eight o'clock, but Mom's getting ready for bed when I go upstairs. Her makeup is washed off, and she looks like a balloon that's deflated after it bounced all around the room with the air whooshing out.

I grab my hairbrush and run it through my bangs in front of the mirror on the door. Frizzy and hopeless. I put on a quick coat of watermelon Chapstick and look again. Better. I grab my binder and head downstairs.

I check the stove burner when I pass it. She turned it off.

Zig is standing on a leather chair in the den, reaching as high as he can, and dropping leaves to the ground. He doesn't even look up when I come in. I put on lip balm for this? I pull a chair to the table and sit down.

"Okay. So I have twenty-five now. I just have to identify them," I tell him, looking for the binder pocket where I tucked the leaves.

"My leaf guide's right there if you want it." Zig bends

down from his chair and brushes aside a pile of leaves on the table. He chooses a big brownish one, steps gingerly from the chair up onto the table, and reaches up again.

"What are you doing?" I ask his sneaker, which is planted firmly on the leaf guide.

"Trying to see if they all flutter or just some of them. You always hear about leaves fluttering to the ground, but I'm thinking that it's really just a phenomenon of the lobed leaves. These other ones seem to do more of a plunging spiral."

He drops the brown one. There is no fluttering whatsoever. I catch it in midair.

"Hey!" Zig frowns at me. "You messed up my experiment."

"They're easier to catch inside."

"Yeah, well . . . that's not how it works."

I hand back the brown, nonfluttering leaf. "What is this one?"

"Catalpa," Zig says.

"God bless you."

He tries not to smile, but his eyes give him away.

"Ha! Made you laugh!"

Zig jumps down from the table, scoops up his leaf pile, and sits down next to me.

"Enough Gee-foolery. Now . . . American elm, cottonwood, linden, honey locust . . ."

"Mr. Nelson said that one was a Kentucky coffee tree."

"It's not. Look." He shows me the page in the leaf guide, and he's right. Kentucky coffee leaves are bigger. Mr. Nelson isn't going to be happy about this.

Zig deals out the leaves in a row in front of me, like cards.

"I have a full house!" I joke.

He ignores me and points to the first leaf. He brushes his hair from his eyes. He frowns, and his forehead wrinkles. "Write it down at least, Gee."

I pick up a pencil and an index card and copy down the scientific name.

"Okay, have you looked up the geographic distribution for this one yet?"

I have. And I wrote it down. And then it got washed off my card, down the shower drain. I sigh and look away from Zig, out the window.

It's too much right now. Too much to add to a vicious fashion-model wannabe trying to steal my spot at sectionals, a mother acting like a robot on too much caffeine, and a grandmother who doesn't know the difference between a watch and a wall clock. My eyes start to sting and I put my head down. I'm *not* going to cry in front of Zig. A warm hand settles on my shoulder lightly, and then goes away. Then it settles again. Warm.

"Gianna," he starts, but the door creaks open, interrupting him. The hand goes away again.

"She's had a long day, sweetie." I hear Nonna's voice and blink away the tears so I can sit up. If anyone's had a long day, it's her.

"Hi, Mrs. DiCarlo." Zig stands to pull up a chair for her, but Nonna shakes her head. "I figured it might have been a tough doctor's appointment when Gianna never called me back. My mom says you should let us know if you need anything." Nonna nods.

"I'm going to get a cookie if that's okay," Zig says, heading for the door. "Want one?"

I shake my head, and he walks out.

"Pretty quiet kitchen after dinner," I say to Nonna.

"It's a lot to think about, Gianna. And sometimes I think things like this are hardest on people like your mom."

"Hard on her?" I know my voice is getting louder, but I can't help it. "She didn't even manage to show up for your appointment!"

"And I thank you for being there for me. It was uncomfortable, to say the least, and it was nice to have an ally."

Nonna walks up behind my chair and pulls out my ponytail holder. I love it when she plays with my hair. She's the only one who can deal with my frizzy tangles.

"I didn't mean it that way," I say.

"I know exactly how you meant it." Nonna separates three sections to start a French braid. "And I'd be angry, too. You talk with your mom about that later on. But for now, just try to understand that she's hurting and she doesn't know what to do with it."

"Do with what?"

"Any of it." She carefully adds more hair to my braid. "You and I, well, we wear everything right out on our sleeves. When we're happy, we sing—loud and out of key sometimes—but we sing. When we're sad, we cry and we think about things, and then we bake some cookies—"

"Or draw a picture," I say.

"Or draw a picture or make a collage or splatter paint on the wall."

"You saw that, huh?"

"It's hard to miss if the stuffed animals fall down." She smiles. "But you keep splattering because it's important. You and I sort out our feelings, and until they're sorted out, we just let them roam around in our souls. Your mom can't do that. The lines in her world are straighter and heavier, and her colors don't really blend. She has to keep things a certain way." Nonna tugs a strand of hair from behind my right ear to make it reach the braid. "And some things don't fit that way."

"Like today." I hand Nonna the ponytail holder and she twists it onto the end of the braid.

"Like today," she says. "She hates that she can't fix it, Gianna."

"So do I."

"I know." I feel Nonna pull gently on a piece of hair that's escaped from my braid to tuck it in. It springs back out, and she leaves it alone.

"How is it that *you're* okay with this?" I can't imagine how hard it must be for Nonna to know she's losing pieces of herself.

"I'm not." She picks up the catalpa leaf and twirls it in a wrinkled hand. Her wedding ring gleams under the desk lamp. "When you've all gone to bed at night, I think about it." She looks out the window. The yellow rectangles of Mrs. Warren's windows glow, and she passes by with a book in her hand. "I look at you and Ian, and I can't imagine there ever being a day when I don't know you and love you. I can't imagine seeing you"—she tucks the catalpa leaf into my braid—"and not knowing every little thing about you. I can't—I just—" Her voice cracks and she looks out the window again. Mrs. Warren's living-room light clicks off.

"I know." I've thought about it too. "But you're here now."

"Most of the time." She sighs. "I drift. But I'm here most of the time."

It hadn't occurred to me that Nonna would see it that way. Going away and coming back. I nod. "It's like this poem we did in English, 'Birches.' "

Nonna wipes a tear from her cheek and smiles a little. "When I see birches bend from left to right . . ."

"You know it?"

"It's my favorite. 'So was I once myself a swinger of birches, and so I dream of going back to be.' "

" 'And when I'm weary of considerations, and life is too much like a pathless wood,' " Zig says quietly. I hadn't heard him come back in.

"Today was a pathless wood day," I say, and Nonna smiles. "And there's that part about going away from earth and coming back again. It's sort of like us. My daydreaming, and your . . . your whatever it is."

"But you know the best line in that poem? 'Earth's the right place for love.' " Nonna takes a deep breath. "That's why I'm trying not to curse the universe too much. I'd rather write down my recipes so they don't get lost. I'd rather bake my cookies and take my walks and visit with my friends, because those are the things I can do right now. If it turns out I can't pick up an eggplant by myself anymore, well . . ."

"We can help pick out eggplants," I say. And Zig nods.

Nonna looks like she's thinking.

"You have to poke them a little. Press into the eggplant with your finger," she says, "and if it springs right back, then it's ripe."

"Got it," Zig says.

"I always knew you were a keeper." Nonna smiles a little and yawns. "I'm turning in. It's been a long one." She kisses me on the cheek. "Sleep well. Tomorrow will be a better day."

I sure hope so.

I watch her leave and turn to Zig, back at his leaf experiments.

He climbs onto his chair with a maple leaf, stretches to the ceiling, and lets it drop.

This one flutters to the wood floor.

CHAPTER 18

Nonna was right. Today is better.

Dad has an early pickup, so I arrive at school in Mom's minivan like every other kid in America. For once, I have everything I need for the day. I checked my assignment book after breakfast. Thursday's boxes are all blank except for science, where I've written "25 LEAVES!!!!!" in humongous letters. And I have them. All twenty-five. I counted twice.

Zig has a dentist appointment in the morning, so I don't see him until after lunch.

"Hey, you're back!" I run to catch him at his locker before science class.

"Hey, Gee. Mom rushed me back so I could check in with Mrs. Loring. Leaf deadline today, you know."

"Yep—twenty-five leaves."

"Collected and identified." Zig slams his locker closed and starts walking, but I freeze.

"Identified?"

"Yeah. We had to have them all identified for today so she can let us know if we need to go back and check any of them before the final project's due tomorrow."

"But I thought we just had to have them."

"Don't tell me you've missed another deadline, Gianna." Bianca swoops over from her locker on the other side of the hall. I swear she has supersonic hearing. "I can't imagine *how* anyone could still be working on this project with all the time we've had, but I guess things happen, don't they?" Her pink lips curl up in a smile. "Don't worry. I've totally got you backed up if you have to miss sectionals." She ducks in front of us into class.

I watch her ponytail swing down the aisle to her seat in back. I'm having fantasies about chopping it off with Nonna's big garden shears when Zig brings me back to reality.

"You didn't identify the rest after I left, huh?"

"Nope. I still have fifteen to go."

"Oh."

"Yeah."

"Well, we better go sit down."

I follow him into class and sink into my seat.

Nonna was wrong. It's not a better day.

The bell rings to start science class, and I pray for a miracle. Mrs. Loring is about to check our leaves. Is it too selfish to ask God to slap some labels on them in my backpack?

"Okay," Mrs. Loring says, passing out the field guides. "Today, you should have all of your leaves identified. I'll let you know if you need to double-check any of them before—"

"Attention teachers and staff," our vice principal, Mr. Yando, booms over the loudspeaker. He's not God, but he'll do. "This is a drill. At this time, please enter lockdown mode and remain there until I come back on the announcements in a little while. This is only a drill."

Mrs. Loring can't find her keys to lock the doors like she's supposed to. By the time she finds them, two school safety officers have come to the wide-open door, shaking their heads. Finally, we're lined up, sitting on the floor in the dark.

I smell perfume and realize I'm next to Mary Beth Rotwiller. She's managed to bring her purse over to the wall and is filing her nails in the light coming in from under the door. She pulls out a second nail file and hands it to Bianca. Mrs. Loring is right next to them but doesn't say anything. It looks like she's either meditating or has fallen asleep.

Mary Beth sees me looking at her and mouths the word "loser" with so much expression I can make it out even in the dark.

I squint to see if I can find Zig. I'm pretty sure that's his shape over by the bookshelf, so I crabwalk across the carpet.

"Hey," I say, looking around as my eyes adjust to the dark.

"No talking," Zig whispers. "You'll get in trouble."

"I know. But it's kind of dumb, don't you think?" I lean against the bookshelf as my eyes adjust to the dark.

"Dumb? Do you have any idea how many raging, gun-toting lunatics have broken down classroom doors in rural Vermont schools because they thought they might have heard whispering inside?"

I let out a snort, and Mrs. Loring's eyes snap open. It's too dark for her to know who to scold, though.

A triangle of tightly folded notebook paper lands in my lap, and I hear Bianca giggle over by the door.

I unfold it.

"Who is crinkling that paper?" Mrs. Loring hisses, so I have to unfold super slow and quiet, until I can finally hold the paper to the light creeping in under the door to read it.

> *Cheer up. Maybe Coach will still let you run the stopwatch at sectionals.* ☺

There's a little smiley next to it. An evil smiley like the one I'd like to wipe off her face right now if it wouldn't make too much noise during the lockdown.

"Look!" I thrust the note at Zig.

He studies it for a minute. More than a minute. Five, maybe. It's hard to tell in the dark.

"Can't you still do it?" he whispers finally.

"Do what?"

"Identify the leaves."

"This isn't about leaves anymore!" I start to raise my voice. "This is about a stuck-up, sparkle-shirt-wearing witch who's trying to steal my spot . . . steal my life! *Look* at this!" I grab the note from him and the paper crackles in the dark.

"Shhh!" Mrs. Loring hisses.

And it's quiet again. I try not to breathe too loud.

"Gee?" I feel Zig's hand on my elbow. Warm. And the mad drains right out of me.

"Sorry."

" 'S'okay. But here's the thing . . ."

"What?"

"It *is* about the leaves."

I sigh. "I know."

"Because if you just finish the project, she goes away."

Zig is going to make someone a fabulously annoying father someday.

"She doesn't, actually. She'll never go away." I watch her toss a football-folded note to Mary Beth. "But I know you're right. I just need to finish it."

Someone rattles the door handle and I jump. The safety monitor must be checking the classrooms now. When they're done, we'll turn the lights on and have science. Zig's rough sweater scratches against my arm.

"I just couldn't think about leaves after you left," I tell him, leaning closer.

"I figured." He pauses. "Do they know if it's Alzheimer's?"

"No, and I'm not sure if they'll ever know a hundred percent. I guess they can test and find out if it's probably Alzheimer's or probably not. But I think Nonna already knows. She said she has a feeling."

"And Nonna's feelings are always right," Zig says. He's been around Nonna long enough to know she has serious intuition. "Well, almost always, anyway. There's that whole wedding thing."

I'm glad it's dark because my face is as red as a sugar maple in October.

Zig pulls his calculator from his backpack and starts fiddling with it while I drift off, out the window, wishing it were time for cross-country.

My right foot has been asleep for almost half an hour when the loudspeaker clicks on.

"Faculty, staff, students. Thank you for your patience. This lockdown drill took longer than anticipated because of some confusion on the lower level of the building, but you all handled yourselves very well. You'll be dismissed for the day when the bell rings."

When the lights come on, Bianca tosses me one last sneer over her shoulder and heads for the door, smoothing the wrinkles out of her skirt.

I look up at the clock.

2:34.

Yes! One minute until science class ends.

No time to check leaves.

Thank you, God and Mr. Yando!

Mrs. Loring looks like she'd like to jump through the loud-speaker and throttle someone in the office, but I'm so happy I try to jump up, straight from sitting pretzel-style to stand-ing. When I land on my right foot, a thousand needles attack it and I stumble into the bookshelves. A thick yellow book teeters off the top shelf and is about to land on my head when Zig snatches it from the air. It's like he was just waiting to save my life. Maybe this will be the beginning of one of those romantic stories. Zig hands me the book that we'll remember someday as the one that started it all. *Tree Identi-fication for Dummies*.

So much for a romantic story.

I start to put the book back on the shelf, but Zig grabs my arm.

"This is perfect for you!" He looks at my face, then down at the book. "I didn't mean it that way. But you should sign one out for tonight. She said we could borrow any of the resources."

"I guess." I pick up the two-inch pencil that Mrs. Loring

has wrapped in duct tape and attached to a string. *Gianna Z,* I write. *Tree Identificaton for Dummies.* There's no denying it. Only a dummy would have waited this long. I have less than a day to identify, write up, and creatively display twenty-five leaves.

CHAPTER 19

By the time I dress for cross-country practice and head out into the afternoon sun, I feel like I can do it. I really think I can do it. I just need to focus. Which isn't exactly my thing, but this time, I'm going to focus if it kills me, because having Bianca Rinaldi running in my place would kill me for sure. I'd drop dead of shame, and she'd probably stand over me in her sparkly T-shirt and say, "Oh, isn't that too bad?"

It's not happening.

I'm going straight home after practice, and I'm going to spend the whole night identifying those leaves and putting them in that dumb binder Mom got me.

I'm getting my leaf project done.

I just am.

But first, I'm going to run.

I take a deep breath, round the corner of the building on the sidewalk that leads out back, and stop like I've run into a wall.

"Well, thanks for your understanding, Bianca. You've certainly been a trouper." Coach Napper takes a paper from Bianca and tucks it into her folder. "I have your permission slip all set, so if things don't work out with—"

Coach stops talking when she sees me.

"If things don't work out?" I say, stepping up to them. I feel my cheeks getting red, and I haven't even started running.

Coach shifts her folder to her other arm. "It's just in case you're . . . not available, Gianna." Bianca smirks.

I step up to her. "What did you tell her?"

Bianca's eyes go all wide. "Just that I was worried about you. I told Coach you're behind on your project, and I knew you'd want the team to have a backup in case you can't go to sectionals."

I turn to Coach. "You don't think I can do it, do you?" I've run with Coach Napper for years—back when she used to do intramurals at Orchard Elementary School, and we could only run from the slides to the swings out on the playground. I always won. How could she stand here telling Bianca she might get to run in my place?

I want to be angry; I really do. I want to grab that stupid folder with the runner lists and the times and meet records and throw it, because it doesn't make a difference anyway. Not if she's going to stick some jogging cover girl in my spot.

But I do what I always do instead. I blink, really fast, to keep from crying. When the tears spill out anyway, I look down. They make little dark splotches in the dirt.

"Gianna . . ." I feel Coach's hand on my shoulder. She squeezes me toward her, but I pull away. "Gianna, it's sectionals. I know you're working on your project, and I'm sure you'll get it done, but . . . I have to make sure we're covered. Bianca's been very understanding about training for a meet where she may not be needed."

"Absolutely, Coach." Bianca flashes a toothpaste-commercial smile and tucks her hair behind her ears as Ellen jogs up.

"Coach, I really need to talk with you about this water-bottle situation."

"No problem." Bianca waves. "I'm off to see if I can knock a few more seconds from my time so I'll be ready for sectionals if the team needs me." She steps past Coach and says, "And I'm *sure* the team will need me." Then she runs off toward the bleachers.

I turn to Coach, but she's already talking with Ellen. "Seriously? We toss more than two million plastic bottles an hour? Sure, I can see how the booster club might support this. Let's see . . . they have a meeting . . ." She didn't hear what Bianca said. Of course, she didn't hear. Bianca is the best at being Snow White in front of teachers and the evil witch behind their backs.

Even though she's off jogging with Mary Beth, her words drift back to me. "And I'm *sure* the team will need me."

In your dreams, Barbie. That's what I should have said, but of course I just stood there. I ought to run after her now that the voice in my head has something good to say.

I'm about to take off when I hear another voice in my head. Zig's.

If you just finish the project, she goes away.

That's what I need to do. And I can.

"Coach?"

"Yeah?" She looks a little nervous about talking to me again, like I might lose it. I surprise her when I smile and say, "Thanks for taking care of my backup, but you're not going to need her. I promise. What was my best time for the four-mile loop last week?"

"Twenty-seven minutes, ten seconds. Why?"

"I just feel like pushing it today." And I take off for the run that has to fuel me through a full night of leaf identification.

The sun plays hide-and-seek, coming and going, lighting the trees, then flickering off. My feet crunch over the gravel to the end of the track, pound the new blacktop of Bridge Street, which still smells like tar. They crackle over dry leaves when I turn onto the dirt path along the river back to school. The leaves are under my feet where they belong—not cluttering up my head—and it's the best run I've had all week.

Twenty-five minutes and forty-five seconds after I started, I slow to a jog back at school and hand over my stopwatch.

"Not bad." Coach grins at me.

"Not bad?"

"Okay, in all honesty, it's the best of the day by a good forty-five seconds. You're still our ringer if you're eligible for sectionals."

"I'll be eligible."

I turn for the locker room just as Bianca comes jogging back onto the track. She stops to fix her hair before she stretches, leaning in to try and hear the end of our conversation.

I make it easy on her.

"No problem, Coach," I say, loud and clear. "I'll finish that leaf project if I have to stay up all night."

CHAPTER 20

Zig waits for me after chess club. He gives me a pep talk as
we walk home.

"You can do this."

I nod. "I'm not looking forward to it, but I'm ready."

"You can do it."

I nod.

"You already have all your leaves."

I nod.

"Look—a black walnut tree!" He points.

I turn. I've seen this particular black walnut before. As a
matter of fact, I've vandalized it. Even if it was unintention-
ally. I shake my head.

"That's Mr. Randolph's house, and there's a fence." I point.

"Gotcha," Zig says. "Only a real dummy would hop his
fence just for a few leaves."

I nod. I have the book in my backpack to prove it.

"Gianna!" My mother is standing on the front porch in her
socks, squinting up the street, like she's looking for something
behind us. I turn around, but no one's there.

"Have you seen Nonna?" she asks. The wrinkles at the
outside corners of her eyes look deeper than usual.

"We're just getting home, Mom. No."

Mom squints past us again, then looks up the street the other way.

"Dad says she left two hours ago to bring cookies to the Jamisons' house up the block, and she's not back. I figured she stayed to chat with Mrs. Jamison, but then Mrs. Jamison came in to meet with Dad about the service tomorrow. She says Nonna left her house more than an hour ago."

My stomach loops in a knot. Where is she?

"Do you want us to walk the neighborhood and see if anyone has seen her?" Zig asks. He loves Nonna almost as much as I do.

"Yes," Mom says. I stand still for a minute and watch her. I can't decide how scared to be. Mom bites her top lip and twists her wedding ring around and around on her finger, looking down from the porch. Finally, she takes a deep breath and nods.

"Just take a quick walk around this block and the next one up toward the store," she says, taking my backpack and heading inside. "I'm going to call the Bensons in case she's there."

Zig starts down the steps but I feel frozen in place. What if something's really happened to Nonna?

Zig looks up at me from the sidewalk. If something is wrong, we need to find her fast. I take the steps two at a time, and we start up the street.

"Let's head up toward the store and swing around back," he says. "Then we can check back here with your mom if we don't find her." He walks faster.

If we don't find her.

We have to find her.

She has to be okay.

A siren blares in the distance, and I start to run, even though I'm not sure where I'm going.

Zig rushes to catch up to me.

"We'll find her, Gee."

I stop so fast he almost crashes into me. "Wait! What if she's at the hospital? Maybe she fell, and someone took her there. Mom should call the hospital and check. We should go back and tell her."

Zig takes my hand and pulls me off the curb. "No, we told her we'd go by the store and check this block. We should do that first." He starts to let go of my hand, but I hold on. I need to hold on to something right now.

A gust of wind whooshes through the treetops over our heads. The leaves swish and rain down in noisy colors onto the sidewalk, and we run all the way to the corner, looking up and down the street.

I need her to be here.

I need her to be safe.

I need to see her walking along with a friend or stepping out of the store with a pint of cream.

But she's not.

"Zig, where would she even be? She's not going to be standing in the middle of the street, and if she fell on the sidewalk, someone would have stopped and helped her."

"Let's check in at the store. Maybe somebody will have seen her."

We start walking again just as the clouds open up. Big, dark spots plunk down on the dappled gray sidewalk. It's cold fall rain that reminds me what winter is going to feel like. I look up, and a drop plops onto my cheekbone. I reach up to wipe it with my palm and realize the chilly raindrop is mixed with the warm, salty water of spilling-over tears. Why didn't Mom and Dad notice sooner that she was gone?

Zig looks over at me. "She's going to be okay, Gee."

"You don't know that!" I drop his hand. "Anything could have happened by now. She could be hurt somewhere, she could have had an accident down by the stream if she decided to walk the back way, she could be . . ."

He takes my hand back. "She's okay." And he pulls me toward the store.

She's okay.

She's okay.

I keep saying it to myself, willing my feet to move in front of one another again.

She's okay. We'll walk up to the store, we'll keep our eyes open, we'll ask around, and if we don't find her, we'll head home. She's probably back there by now. I'll think positive. She probably ran into one of her friends from church out gardening and then stopped to see her chrysanthemums and popped in for a cup of tea and lost track of time. She's probably home by now, starting dinner. I'm breathing more slowly, and the tears have stopped, but my hair and clothes are soaked. The rain has picked up.

We fly up the steps of the Corner Mart. There's still no sign of Nonna, and the sky is starting to rumble.

Zig pulls open the door, and the bell jingles as we step in, dripping on the gray tiles. Mr. Mulcahy looks up from the cash register where he's ringing up a box of cereal for Ruby and her mom.

"Gianna! You look like an Irish setter that's just had a cold shower." Normally, I'd joke right back with Mr. Mulcahy; today I don't even notice. I don't answer him. I don't even say hi to Ruby or ask how she's doing. I just stand there with my hair dripping into my eyes.

Mr. Mulcahy rips off two paper towels from the roll behind the deli counter and hands them to me.

"Has Gianna's grandmother been in lately, Mr. Mulcahy?" Zig asks.

Mr. Mulcahy shakes his head and turns to me. "You're looking for her?"

"She's . . . We can't find her. I mean, she's okay. I think she is. I hope she is. But she went to see Mrs. Jamison and left hours ago and isn't home yet." I start to cry again. Without saying anything, Ruby sets down the Cheerios and puts a hand on my shoulder. Mr. Mulcahy comes out from behind the counter.

"Have your folks called the police?"

"No. Well, maybe, by now. We're checking the neighborhood first."

The sky outside flashes, and the whole store lights up. Two seconds later, thunder booms so loud it rattles the cans of tuna fish on the shelves.

"This isn't weather for anyone to be out in." Mr. Mulcahy frowns. He reaches under the counter for his keys. "I'll run you two home in the delivery van. It's time to close up anyway, and we can check any streets where you haven't looked for your grandmother yet."

"I'll go with you!" Ruby looks at her mom after she says it. I'm not sure what good it will do to have her along, but somehow just the fact that she offered makes it seem like there's hope. Ruby's mom nods and reaches into her pocket for a cell phone.

"Call if you're not going to be home by five thirty." She kisses Ruby on the forehead and stops to take my hand. "You call too, if your family needs anything at all."

When Mr. Mulcahy swings open the glass door, the rain is roaring, like static on television turned up full blast. The maple leaves on the sidewalk look wet and dark.

Zig opens the door to the red delivery van parked by the curb. I climb in and scoot over to make room for him and Ruby. The three of us all scrunch into the front seat, and it doesn't leave much room for Mr. Mulcahy, but he squeezes in, buckles his seatbelt, and makes a quick U-turn in front of the store.

"Anywhere you want me to drive so we can take a look?" he asks, turning the windshield wipers up to full blast.

"I don't think so." I sigh. I don't know where else to look, or even how we'd see Nonna in all this rain. It's like wet, gray curtains. "Could you just drop us at my house and I'll see if my parents have any news?"

But before we get to my block, I spot a tall, wet woman in a business suit running down the sidewalk toward us.

"That's my mom!"

Mr. Mulcahy beeps the horn and stops. She runs up to his window.

"Nonna is at the Simmonses' house." Her wet hair is plastered to her face. "Come with me. I may need your help."

"Mom, Ruby's here too. She was at the store when Zig and I—"

"I don't care who comes. Let's go!"

"Thanks, Mr. Mulcahy." We jump down from the van. I walk around to Mom, expecting to see relief on her face, but the creases around her eyes are still there. She starts jogging again. Zig and Ruby and I have to run to catch up.

"She's okay, right?" I ask, starting to breathe more quickly. Mom is moving fast, and her legs are longer than ours.

"She's okay," Mom says, but not like she means it. We cross the street to get to the Simmonses' house. I expect Mom to go right up to the front door, but she whips around the side porch and heads for their pool out back. I follow her but stop short when I reach the open gate and see why she came this way. Ruby and Zig stop right behind me.

Nonna is sitting on the edge of the pool with her feet in the water, soaking wet from head to foot. She must be freezing. I can't tell if she fell in or if she's just been out in the rain all afternoon, but she's looking up at Mrs. Simmons like she's terrified of her, even though she's known her for years. Mrs. Simmons is soaked too. She looks relieved when Mom runs up.

I'm still at the gate and can't hear what Mrs. Simmons says, but Mom listens, and I see her reach up to wipe water from her eyes when she looks over at Nonna, sitting on the edge of the pool. Her feet are still in the water with her beige orthopedic shoes tied neatly. She's still staring up at Mrs. Simmons and Mom, like they're aliens.

It looks like a scene from a movie. A scene from somebody else's family. Mine is supposed to be home, watching the rain from the window and eating funeral-wedding cookies and arguing over homework.

"Why does she look like that?" I whisper.

"She's confused," Zig says, stepping closer to me. His wet sweatshirt brushes my arm. "But she's okay. Your mom's taking care of her."

Mom walks over to Nonna, squats down next to her, and puts a hand on her shoulder. Nonna listens, but she still looks lost.

I shiver. Now that I'm not running, the wind chills me through my soaked clothes and my nose is running. I wipe it on my sleeve, wrap my arms around myself, and look down at Mrs. Simmons's planters by the swimming-pool gate. They're full of yellow mums, too bright and out of place. They ought to quiet down and turn brown like everything else.

When I look up, Nonna is finally letting Mom help her to her feet. They start walking toward the gate, toward us, and step out of the pool area just as Dad pulls the van into the driveway. Ian jumps out of the backseat and runs to Mom.

"I'm going to talk with Mrs. Simmons for just a minute. Go tell Daddy we'll be right there. And take this to the car for me." She hands Ian her cell phone, and his eyes light up. He races to the car. Ruby and Zig follow him, but I stay back.

I turn to Nonna. She's staring at the minivan as if she's never seen it before. Finally, I reach out for her hand. She looks down at my hand, takes it, and looks into my eyes. "Gianna," she says, and I realize I've been holding my breath.

I breathe out now. She knows who I am. She may not know where she is. She may not know the green Honda Odyssey. But Nonna knows me.

"Come on, Nonna." Dad's waiting to help her into the backseat.

I get in on the other side and climb over Ruby and Zig so I can sit next to Nonna.

"Hello, Kirby," Nonna says. She knows Zig, too, even if she's forgotten he hates to be called by his real name.

"Hi, Nonna. Good to see you."

"And who's your new friend?" Nonna asks, nodding at Ruby.

"You know Ruby, Nonna."

"Ruby? Are you one of the nurses at Dr. Hebert's office?"

Ruby bites her lip and shakes her head. I stare straight ahead at the raindrops on the windshield and try not to cry.

"Ruby's my friend from school, Nonna." And you were the one who convinced me of that, I think. You were the one who dragged me to her grandmother's funeral. You told me I had to be there for her, and you don't even remember her now.

"Well, hello, Ruby, the friend from school."

"It's nice to meet you." Ruby reaches across me to shake Nonna's hand, and water drips from her sleeve into my lap. Nonna makes a *tsk*ing sound with her tongue.

"You're going to catch your death of cold, Ruby." She looks at my wet curls and Zig's dripping hair. "And so are the two of you. What were you thinking, going out without a raincoat in this weather?"

I don't have an answer for her. Ian leans over from his seat and takes a picture of the four of us, dripping quietly.

Mom gets in. We ride home. No one speaks.

Except Nonna. She looks out the window. "What a gully-washer!"

CHAPTER 21

Thanks so much. Everything's just fine now. Bye, Ruby! Take care, sweetheart!"

Mom watches Ruby get into her mom's car and ride away.

"Do you want to call your mom?" she asks Zig. "I could give you a ride home."

"No, I'll walk; the rain stopped." He turns to me. "Call me if you need help later."

"Okay. Thanks." But I can't imagine thinking about leaves tonight, and suddenly, sectionals seem a whole lot less important.

Mom waves to Zig before she closes the door. We climb the stairs to the kitchen, where Nonna's waiting.

"You." Mom points to me. "Go work on your leaf collec- tion." She points up the stairs to my bedroom. My father stares at us, three generations of dripping women, with question marks in his eyes.

"Mom, how can I—"

"It's due tomorrow, right?"

I nod.

"Then go." Mom flicks her wrist up the stairs over and

over, like she's trying to shake off a bee that's stinging her. "I need to get dinner started." She sloshes across the kitchen floor and pulls a package of chicken from the refrigerator. Nonna walks in and sits down on the sofa. Her gray curls are plastered to her forehead. She takes off her wet sweater and drapes it carefully over the back of the couch.

"Let's see," Mom says to the refrigerator. "Carrots or broccoli? Carrots, I think."

Dad looks from Mom, standing in her puddle on the linoleum, to Nonna on the couch. His eyes rest on me.

"Go on upstairs, Gianna," he says quietly. It's the quiet that makes me explode.

"Is everyone going to keep pretending nothing just happened?" I storm into the living room. My sneakers make dark tracks on the beige carpet, but I don't care. "She's sitting on the couch soaking wet, and everyone's pretending that's perfectly normal. It's not! And I'm not going to go up to my room as if I didn't just spend the whole afternoon out looking for her." I point to Nonna on the couch, and she cringes as if I've hit her. But I keep going. "It's not okay! None of this is okay!" I collapse on the sofa sobbing and bury my face in Nonna's soggy shoulder. After what feels like a long time, I feel a gentle hand on my knee.

I don't want to talk. I keep my head down, but put my hand on top of hers. It feels like birch bark.

"Come on, *bella*." She used to call me that when I was little. It means "beautiful" in Italian, and somehow, it makes me feel a little better.

But her voice sounds very, very tired. "Let's both go get into some dry clothes," she says.

Nonna pads down the hall to her room, leaving soggy footprints all the way, and I go back through the kitchen and upstairs. Mom chops her carrots into smaller and smaller pieces and doesn't even look up.

I change into wind pants and a sweatshirt and feel a little better. Maybe I can identify some leaves. I guess I might as well.

I can't find any of my leaves or books, though. Mom probably threw them out again. My chest tightens and I get madder and madder at her until I remember that I handed her my backpack earlier and everything else is in the den from when I worked with Zig before.

When I open the door to the den, Nonna's sitting at the table in front of my pile of evergreens.

"I found lots of pine trees." I sit down next to her and pick up a stem with extra pointy needles.

"That's not from a pine tree." She takes it from me and holds it to her nose, inhaling deeply. "This one's from a balsam fir." She turns it in her hand, and some of the needles fall to the table. Nonna frowns. "A balsam fir that's been dead for a while. Where did you get this sample?"

"From the Christmas wreath I made in the after-school program last year. The one hanging on my closet door."

"You still have the Christmas wreath on your door?" Nonna raises her eyebrows.

"Well, I was going to take it down, but I kept forgetting, and since it's already October . . ."

Nonna smiles and smells the needles again. Aren't they pricking her nose? She picks up my pencil, scribbles into my notebook, and hands it to me. A poem.

I miss you in the summer,
I miss you in the fall, some,
But specially at Christmas time,
I pine, fir, yew, and balsam.

I groan. "This sounds like one of Ian's riddles. Or a Dad joke."

"I heard that." Dad closes the door behind him and pulls up a chair. "Listen," he says. "I ordered a pizza."

"Pizza from a store? *Che porcherie!*" Food for pigs, she says. Nonna gets up and heads for the kitchen. "I'm getting some tea, and then I'll be back to help you, Gianna. Store pizza . . . ay-yay-ay."

"I thought Mom was making that chicken." I pick up my pencil and start doodling Christmas trees around Nonna's poem.

"Mom needed a little time alone."

"She's crying, isn't she?" The only other time I've ever seen Mom cry was when her best friend from high school died of breast cancer three years ago. We did the calling hours here. Mom zipped around the house with cold-cut platters and cookie trays all day long and scoured the kitchen counter until it gleamed when everyone left. Then she put the sponge down and cried for half an hour.

"She's worn out." Dad picks up the balsam fir, and the rest of the needles fall. He twirls the twig between his fingers. I take it away and put it down.

"Maybe she wouldn't have to cry if she'd talk about what's wrong once in a while."

"Your mom's doing her best with this, Gee, she really is.

Mom likes answers. And right now, everything about Nonna is just a great big question."

"So she takes it out on me." I break the twig in half.

"She doesn't mean to." Dad sighs. "She'll come around. She just needs time to deal with this in her own way. Then she'll be able to help you through it too."

The doorbell rings. "Pizza must be here." He pulls his wallet from his pocket and stands. "Be patient with her, Gee. She'll be back." He leaves to pay for the pizza.

Nonna shuffles back in with her tea, sets it down, and picks up another evergreen sample.

"Now this one," she says, holding up its lacy design. "This one is from a cedar tree. My grandmother—that's your great-great-grandmother—told me she made cedar tea when her mother had cholera back in the 1850s. They had tried all kinds of remedies, but it was the cedar tea that finally cured her."

Magic leaves. I would have been interested in this leaf collection a whole lot earlier if I'd known about the magic ones.

I wonder what would happen if I slipped some cedar into Nonna's tea.

"Dinner!" Dad calls from the kitchen. Nonna picks up her cup and leaves before I can find out.

CHAPTER 22

Dinner is quiet. Only Ian talks. He just got a new Geo-Genius electronic map.

"Gianna, know what the state fish of Hawaii is called?" I shake my head.

"It's the huma huma nuku nuku apua." He emphasizes every syllable, especially the last one. "Hooma-Hooma-Nooka-Nooka-Wah-Pa-Wah-*AH*!"

Normally, we'd all make jokes and ask Ian to spell that name. Tonight, all he gets is a little chuckle from Nonna.

"Which state is called the Show Me State?"

"Pennsylvania?" Mom guesses. Her eyes are still red, but she's eating her pizza.

"Nope. Missouri." Ian grins like he's just won the world geography bee championship.

We take turns guessing the state bird of Idaho, the state motto of Kentucky, and the state tree of Vermont. We guess everything wrong. I suppose some days are like that.

Finally, I finish my pizza and get up to clear my plate. "I'm going to bed."

"Gianna, you—," my mother begins, but my father cuts her off.

"Good night."

"Good night, *bella*." Nonna holds out her hand, and I take it to lean in and kiss her on the cheek before heading upstairs.

I'm just pulling my oversized Monet *Water Lilies* T-shirt over my head when Mom comes in and plops down on the big chair next to my bed. She moves a few stuffed animals to make room, and I squeeze in beside her.

"I guess you know Nonna's condition is serious." She picks up my stuffed kangaroo, Mabel, and pulls her baby out of her pouch.

"I knew before you did." I take Mabel from her and stuff the joey back in Mabel's pocket where it belongs.

"I knew, Gianna. I've known for months."

"Months?"

She nods. "I just didn't want to deal with it until we found out for sure. I guess I kept telling myself that if we just went about our business, things would get better."

"They didn't."

"I know. And I see that now." She picks up Betty, my stuffed Orca whale, and starts playing with her dorsal fin. Finally, she looks up at me. "You realize that if Nonna does have Alzheimer's—"

"She thinks she does."

"I know. And if she's right, it means . . ." She picks up Mabel again, in her other hand. It's a two-animal discussion. Mom takes a deep breath. "She's going to keep slipping away from us, Gee. The writer Elie Wiesel says Alzheimer's disease is like taking a book and ripping out the pages one at a time until all that's left is a cover." She arranges Mabel and Betty on the arm of the chair and looks up at me. "It hurts to think about it."

I nod. "I know. I'm scared she's going to drift off and not come back."

Mom's eyes are wet. "Someday, she will." She takes my hand. "But for now, we're going to do what we can to keep her here with us and keep her safe. Dad's going to the hardware store tomorrow to get an automatic shutoff switch for the stove so it will turn itself off after a couple of hours if it's left on. And we're going to get an alarm for the doors so we know if Nonna's going out."

"You're going to keep her locked inside? That'll kill her, Mom."

"No, no, no . . . But we'll know when she's going and where she's going, so we can help her get home if she needs help."

"She's going to need a lot of help, isn't she?" I ask. Mom stands up and kisses me on the head.

"She has the best helper anyone's ever known. You two are kindred spirits. I know you'll be there for her. And we'll be here for you. Now get into bed."

"I can't—I've still got homework and I have to—"

"Into bed. It's after eleven."

"But Mom—"

"Gianna, you're already exhausted. Go to bed."

I hate it, but she's right. There's no way I can finish identifying those leaves tonight anyway. I'm too tired even to argue.

She scoops up a stack of notebooks that spilled across the floor when I tripped over them on my way in.

"It looks like a tornado hit this room."

"Do you know what state has the most tornadoes, on average, per year?"

"No, but I know someone who does. . . . Want me to call him up here?" She grins at me.

"No, that's okay." I smile back.

She kicks some dirty clothes out of her path and opens the door.

"Get some sleep."

" 'Night."

She takes my backpack with her when she leaves, probably to make sure I don't turn the light back on and work.

I climb into bed, pull the covers up to my chin, and stare at the blue-white rectangle the streetlight makes on my closet door. How can a person be so exhausted and wide-awake all at once?

I reach for the laser pointer on my nightstand and press the button so a little red light appears on the ceiling. If I swish it around fast enough, it leaves a trail of light, like the tail of a comet. I draw slow red lines on the ceiling. A figure eight. A flower blossom. It helps me calm down.

I'm going to be okay. Mom's back from her cleaning and cooking frenzy. Nonna's back from her walk in the rain. Right now, things are okay.

And then I remember that things aren't. Bianca Rinaldi turned in her permission slip. She's all set for sectionals if the team needs her.

And tomorrow is the due date for the leaf collection.

CHAPTER 23

I don't feel good.

My throat hurts.

My stomach feels funny too. Like I might throw up.

Or have diarrhea.

I can't go to school with diarrhea. I'd be running to the bathroom all day.

Maybe I have Dutch elm disease.

I think I should stay home.

I'll just explain to Mom.

CHAPTER 24

Maybe not.

I'm hammering the snooze button into submission for the third time when Mom comes in and pulls back the covers. Her coffee mug is already half empty, but she still looks exhausted.

"Rise and shine!" Normally, it drives me crazy when she says that in her singsong morning voice, but today, she actually sounds like she just means to say hello, so I let it go.

I pull on my fringed jean skirt and a stretchy shirt with Van Gogh's *Starry Night* across the front. Sometimes an outfit I love puts me in a better mood. These blues and golds have special magic. But I doubt even Vincent can help me today.

When I get to the breakfast table, the binder Mom got me for my leaf collection sits next to my Rice Krispies. She can't possibly think I'm going to finish this up during breakfast. She must not have any idea how much work I have left. I finally have all the leaves, and I've jotted down information about them, but nothing is in order. I pick up the binder to move it out of my breakfast space. It's heavy. Really heavy.

I flip open the cover. On the front page, typed on acid-free paper inside a laminated sleeve, is a table of contents listing twenty-five kinds of leaves.

Is it really possible? I flip it over.

Page 1: White Cedar

Page 2: Eastern Hemlock

Page 3: Wild Black Cherry

And the pages go on and on. All the way to twenty-five. Black walnut. I worked hard for that black walnut.

Every page is perfectly arranged with its leaf and the required information plus some extra berries and nuts in little plastic bags for bonus points. The pages are decorated with little leaf stickers. I look up from the project. Mom's smiling at her oatmeal.

"I know it's been a long week, and you really did have most of this project done." She sits down across from me and pats the leaf binder. "I thought I'd just sort of pull it all together for you. You don't want to turn in a sloppy project."

"Thanks," I tell her. I still can't believe what she's done. It must have taken all night. I had never planned on typing up my notes. Every page had a detailed description in twelve-point font.

My stomach stops churning and jumps for joy. It's done. No more moldy leaves. No more dichotomous keys. I can go to school. No lecture on responsibility. No detention. No sparkly T-shirts at sectionals.

"You better get going." Mom swallows a mouthful of oatmeal. "Dad's going to take you in today. He has a pickup at the hospital. Hurry, okay? I think he's already outside."

I put my bowl in the sink and ease the leaf binder into my backpack. It's stuffed so full it barely fits, and it makes the backpack weigh a ton.

I'm afraid to let this project leave my side, so I carry it around in my bag all day. By the time I've schlepped it all the way to ninth-period science class, the strap is cutting into my shoulder. I can't wait to put it down and turn this thing in, once and for all.

"Okay!" Mrs. Loring is standing at her desk, looking like a kid on Christmas morning. "Let's have those leaf collections. You can turn them in on the side table there."

I'm about to go up to the front of the room to put my leaf project in the pile, but I'm mesmerized by the wild variety of the projects passing by my desk. Ellen goes up first to turn hers in—a bulging orange scrapbook full of pressed leaves. Her title page says in huge letters:

ELLEN FRANKENHOFF'S LEAF COLLECTION
CREATED ON 100% RECYCLED PAPER
NO TREES WERE HARMED
IN THE MAKING OF THIS PROJECT

Kevin Richards, whose projects always remind me of Pigpen from *Charlie Brown,* brings up his leaf binder with needles and leaves sticking out all over. A couple slide out and land under my desk as he walks by. I think they're both slippery elm. It figures.

Mary Beth and Bianca go up together to turn in their projects. They have matching purple binders with the word "LEAVES" spelled out in silver and metallic pink on the cover.

Their glue must not have been dry all the way. The glitter sprinkles a little trail behind them on the floor.

Zig is next, carrying a huge roll of newsprint when he walks by. He leans it against Mrs. Loring's desk.

"What's up with the mural?" I whisper as he passes me.

"It's a geographical depiction of my leaves and their distribution in the Western Hemisphere," Zig says. I nod, even though I don't get it. He can always tell when I'm pretending. "I have a giant map of the United States, with the leaves affixed to the actual locations where they're the most common. Along with the relevant information, of course."

"Of course." I nod. He winks at me and heads to his seat.

Ruby walks past next.

"Oh look," Bianca says. "Ruby made one of those poor-kid leaf projects Mrs. Loring talked about—where you don't have to buy a binder or anything." Mary Beth snickers.

"At least hers isn't shedding glitter all over the floor. It's supposed to be a leaf collection—not a self-portrait of your made-up face."

Bianca stares at me like she can't believe the words came out of my mouth. And I guess I can't either. She looks up at Mrs. Loring, but she's busy taking a late pass from Ricky Garcia, who swears it wasn't because his project wasn't done.

"Great project, Ruby." I say it so everyone can hear.

"Thanks." Ruby smiles a little and adjusts one of her index cards, which was crooked.

"Yeah," Ellen says. "It's cool because you made it totally yourself."

A couple other girls in our row nod, and Ruby holds her head a little higher when she sets her project down in the front of the room. She has twenty-five leaves neatly arranged on a piece of cardboard that looks like it might have been part of an appliance box once. The information cards next to each leaf aren't typed, but they're printed in tidy handwriting, and at the bottom of each index card is what looks like a short poem.

She sees me squinting and leans over. "It's haiku," she whispers. "I did one for each leaf."

It's beautiful, but instead of feeling happy for her, I feel sick.

The churning in my stomach is back.

I look down at my leaf collection. Correction. My mother's leaf collection.

The perfectly typed descriptions. The crisp pages. All of it perfect. And none of it mine.

"Does anyone still need to turn in a leaf project?" Mrs. Loring looks around the room.

As soon as her eyes leave me, I slip the leaf binder back into my book bag and kick it under my desk.

Nonna's pulling a tray of cookies from the newly modified oven when I get home, but I don't even stop to get one. I go straight to my room with my book bag, pull out the leaf project and plop it onto my desk. Now what?

I look at my clock radio.

2:44.

Coach gave me permission to miss practice if I run on my own later. She didn't ask why. I think she knew.

I just hope Mrs. Loring is as understanding.

Because technically, the project was due by the end of

school today. Mrs. Loring coaches soccer, so technically, her school day doesn't end until soccer practice is over at five thirty. So technically, I still have time to make something and take it back to school and give it to her before five thirty and have it turned in on time. But what kind of something should I make?

The door opens and Nonna walks in with five perfectly round, rainbow-sprinkled cookies on a plate.

"Bad day?" She sets down the plate on my desk.

"Yeah." There's no use hiding from Nonna. I hand her the binder of leaves. She flips through it and frowns.

"Your mother?"

"Yep."

"She helped you with it?"

"Nope."

"She did your leaf collection herself?" Nonna looks down at the project in her hands and sighs. "You don't even have to answer that. This has Angela written all over it." She flips to the table of contents, where some leaves have subheadings for different varieties.

"I think she was trying to help," I offer weakly.

Nonna laughs a little. "Of course she was trying to help. Just like she was trying to help when she turned into the manic chef the other night."

"After you wandered off? Do you remember all that now?"

She shakes her head and looks down, embarrassed. "No, but we talked about it with the doctor today. Your mom took me back for my blood work."

"Do they know anything?"

"No, Gianna, they don't. And really, whether they decide

they can call it Alzheimer's disease in my case or not, you and I both know that I'm just not . . . here . . . sometimes." Her voice breaks. "I'm afraid," she says very quietly, and a tear runs down from the corner of her eye.

"Me too," I whisper.

I reach out for her hand and hold it. We're quiet for a few minutes.

Finally, Nonna takes a deep breath and lets go of my hand. She flips the leaf binder open to the weeping willow page, running her fingers over its fluttery leaves through the plastic. She turns a page and the gorgeous sugar maple leaf jumps out at us, shining red. It's the one I tried to draw. I came close to that real color, too. Another page. A Norway spruce sticking out the edge of the plastic.

"Careful, it's all prickly. I don't like that one," I tell her, taking another cookie.

"Sometimes, prickly is what you need to get by," Nonna says. She flips through the paper birch and maple pages. "Sometimes you need to dive, and sometimes you need to flutter. And sometimes," she says, turning back to the Norway spruce, "you just need to be tough and hang on."

"You know," I say, taking the binder and flipping through the plastic pages. "I didn't really hate this project. I love how different they all are. They don't just look different; they act different, too." I bite into the last cookie, and the crumbs sprinkle onto the binder.

"Nature is an amazing teacher." Nonna raises her eyebrows, picks up the plate, and heads for the door.

"Hey, wait—" I hold up the binder. "What do you think I should do with this?"

"Those are your leaves in there, Gianna. Your mother made her leaf collection, and it doesn't work for you. Take the leaves back and make your own." She closes the door behind her. I'm left with twenty-five leaves in a plastic three-ring prison and, finally, an idea for how to set them free.

CHAPTER 25

By the time Zig knocks on the door half an hour later, my bedroom carpet looks like a forest floor. The leaves cover almost every square inch. Zig has to tiptoe across the room. He finally finds a leafless patch next to my desk where he can stand.

"Should I ask?" He looks around at the leaves, newly liberated from their tidy binder, and bends down to pick one up.

"Don't touch that!"

"Sorry."

"It's just that they're all in the order I want them. I know it sort of looks like a big disaster in here, but I know what I'm doing now."

Zig squints at me like I'm speaking another language.

Ian's head pops into the doorway. He's wearing a football helmet.

"Hey, do you know what time it is?"

"It's . . . uh . . ." Zig starts to push up his sleeve.

"It's *time* to finish your leaf collection!" Ian laughs, and ducks out of the room.

"That wasn't a very good one!" I shout after him.

"Okay, how's this . . . ? Do you know what time your leaf collection will be done?" He pops back in.

"I give up. Tell us what time and then you have to leave so I can finish."

"At *tree* o'clock!" I grab the roll of tape and throw it at him, but it just bounces off the helmet. He planned ahead.

"Here." I sigh. "Hold this." I hand Zig a sycamore leaf with a long string tied onto the stem. I attach the other end of the string to a hoop I made from an unraveled wire hanger and hand it to Zig. He's still looking at me like I'm nuts.

"You had it done. In the binder. I thought you turned it in."

I shake my head. "It wasn't my binder. It was Mom's."

His eyes get big. "She *did* your project?"

I nod. "It was a long night after you left. Anyway, I'm redoing it. I have to finish and get this to school by five thirty. Help me, and I'll fill you in."

Zig should win a prize for best leaf-collection buddy and best listener. He nods, ties strings, asks questions, and holds seeds while I bring him up to date. By the time I finish the story, the project—my project this time—is almost done.

"There." I climb up on my chair and hold the wire hoop up to the ceiling.

Leaves of every shape and size and color hang down at three different levels. The bottom tier has deciduous leaves—the ones that fall every autumn so new ones can grow in the spring. The middle tier is evergreens, leaves like Nonna that hang in there, season after season. And the top tier is unique. There's just one real leaf—the sugar maple. That's me, I've decided. All around it, I've hung the cutouts of my leaf sketches—the ones I did in colored pencil. They came so close, almost capturing these colors of nature, but not quite. On the back of each leaf, I've glued a note card where I've written in calligraphy pen the common and scientific names of the tree, where it grows, and how it's used. And one last index card for my signature.

Gianna Z.

Now it's a work of art.

I blow a gentle breeze at the mobile and watch. The birch leaf, the color of brushed gold, twirls in a quick circle. Next to it, that prickly Norway spruce hangs a little lower; its dark needles catch the sunlight through my window, and they shine.

"It's perfect." Zig smiles. "It's you."

I stop blowing, and the leaves dangle from their strings. I wish they'd keep moving like they do outside, dipping and twirling in the wind.

"Zig!" He's right next to me, and I say it so loud he jumps and bangs his elbow into my dresser. "Do you have your electrical stuff in your backpack?"

"Yeah, it's behind the door there." He rubs his elbow.

"What would it take to make this whole thing spin around?"

A smile spreads across his face. "A few wires, a nine-volt battery, and a small motor, which I have right in here." He rummages in his backpack until he's found them. "And an electronic genius." He grins. "Just give me a minute."

"Cool." I watch as he starts stripping the ends of the wires. "Do you really think it'll work? I mean, where are you going to attach it? Are they all going to spin? Because really, I want the whole thing to spin."

Zig bites his lower lip and holds the battery up to the light as he attaches a wire.

"Are you going to wrap that around there or do you need a piece of tape or something?" I ask him. "I don't think that looks like it's going to stay, do you? I could get you some tape. I'm thinking that if we taped it, we might be able to attach it up here, and—"

"Gee!" This time, I jump.

"What?"

"Shhh! I can't concentrate."

"I'm just trying to help, because what I really want is for this part here . . ." I point to the deciduous leaves, and Zig grabs my hand. Another little zap of electricity. My hand tingles. I shut up.

"Trust me." He pulls my hand away from the mobile but doesn't let go. His hand is warm. Not sweaty or anything. Just nice and warm. From the battery maybe.

"Close your eyes," he says. I do. My heart beats like it's going to thump right out of my chest and keep thumping across my desk. And it thumps even faster when I remember that this is exactly how kisses always start in movies, with the whole closed eyes thing. Is he going to kiss me? I'm not ready for this. I wish I'd put on some Chapstick. I'm thinking about opening my eyes for a peek, when he drops my hand, and I hear him rummaging through his bag again.

"Can I open them?"

"When I'm done. I just need to find the right apparatus."

This is not a kissing kind of conversation. And there's an awful lot going on. Scratchy wire sounds, rustling leaves, ripping noises, and finally a whirring sound like I heard at the dentist last time I had to get a tooth filled. Definitely not kissing sounds. I can't decide if I'm relieved or disappointed.

"Okay," Zig says. "Open 'em."

I open my eyes and laugh out loud. My leaf collection is wired up like some kind of crazy nature merry-go-round. Zig has reshaped the hanger, duct-taped a battery to it, and wired the battery to a small motor mounted in the middle of the mobile. The whole thing is set up to twirl around in circles when you turn it on.

"You do the honors." He points to a little black toggle switch on the motor.

I flip the switch and my leaf collection springs to life. The sycamore dances with the cedar, and the white oak waltzes with the willow. It's poetry in motion. A whirling dervish. And so totally me.

My door opens and Mom walks in.

"Gianna, do you have homework tonight, because—" My cyclone of a leaf collection stops her cold. Zig reaches over and turns it off, but I flip it back on. We might as well have this conversation now.

"What happened to your binder?" Her eyes follow the leaves in little circles.

"Here." I hold it up, empty. "I love that you stayed up all night to help me, Mom, and it was beautiful. It was all you, though." I gesture toward the mobile. "This one's me."

Mom bites her lip, watching my eastern hemlock get tangled up in the red oak. She doesn't say anything, though. Nonna walks into the room, looks at my leaf mobile for a minute, and smiles.

"Well done." She looks at the twirling leaves, squints at

the gadget that's set them in motion, and nods in Zig's direction. "He's a keeper, this one." My face gets all warm.

Nonna puts her hand on Mom's elbow and leads her out of the room. She closes the door, but I can hear her voice in the hall.

"Come on, Angela, let's go have a cookie."

Zig high-fives me, and I start gathering the leaf crumbs littered all over my floor. I bend to pick up a beech leaf and smile. Nonna may be slipping away, but she's still right about so many things.

My leaf mobile is still twirling and twirling, and some more leaves are twisted together. Zig reaches over to free them.

"The sugar maple's gotten all tangled up with the red oak." Zig brushes his hair from his eyes and grins.

Maybe Nonna will even be right about us.

Zig points to the clock.

5:15.

"Don't you have someplace to be with that leaf mobile?"

I nod and reach for my running shoes. "You coming?"

"Wouldn't miss it for anything."

Cross-country and soccer practices are both wrapping up when Zig and I come flying down the sidewalk.

"Looks like you've started your workout already!" Coach Napper says. "Is it done?"

I nod. It's better than done. It's brilliant. I hold it up to show her, and she grins.

"We're winding down, but you can do a few miles on your own after you get home. Soccer's done, too. You just caught her." She points toward the soccer field where Mrs. Loring is collecting the practice balls into a big mesh bag. "She stopped by at the beginning of practice to tell me your project wasn't in. I told her you'd be back. She's expecting you."

"Did she say if she'd count it on time?"

"Well." Coach smiles. "She was going to dock you a letter grade, but I told her that technically she'd said it was due at the end of the school day, and since *her* school day doesn't end until soccer practice is over, then technically . . ."

"Technically, you are the greatest coach in the universe. Thanks!"

Zig shuffles over to the school steps to wait, and I run to Mrs. Loring. I have to keep slowing down so my leaves don't get tangled.

"Gianna Z. . . . the last unchecked box on my leaf-collection chart. You made it." She smiles, ties the bag of soccer balls shut, flings it over her shoulder, and nods toward the storage shed. "Walk with me."

I have to take three steps to every one of hers because my legs are so much shorter. "Thanks," I say. "I really needed the extra time to make sure my project was . . . mine."

She opens the shed door, tosses the balls inside, slams it shut, and reaches for my leaf project. "Let's see."

The wind dies down, so the leaves hang just like they're supposed to. "White oak, paper birch, American beech . . ." She lifts each leaf gently so she can read the card that hangs below it. "Very nice work," she says finally. "And my gosh—is that a black walnut leaf? That tree is quite rare. Where did you ever get your hands on one?"

"In a neighbor's yard," I mumble.

"What a lovely neighbor for sharing it with you," she says.

I imagine Mr. Randolph screaming from his doorway. "Yep," I say. She really doesn't need to know.

"Well, you did it, Gianna," she says as we approach the school steps where the rest of the cross-country team is stretching. "When I go in, I'll tell Coach Napper her star runner is available for sectionals."

"Thank you!"

"You did the work. And you've certainly earned the right to run. Your times this season have been incredible."

She says it loud enough for the whole team to hear. Including Ellen, who puts down the clipboard with her water bottle petition so she can clap for me. Including Bianca, who looks like she might scream. I take a closer look at her. Her hair is still flawless, and she's wearing her glittery shirt, but she doesn't look perfect to me anymore. I guess it's hard to be pretty when you're about to explode.

"I'll see you on Monday, Mrs. Loring," I say. I can't wait to tell Zig.

"Gianna?"

"Yeah?"

"I just wanted to tell you, I love the way your leaf collection captures your personal style, too." She holds it up and the leaves flutter a little in the wind.

"Style? Hmph!" The snort from the steps only could have come from one person. I walk right up to her. So close that I can read her shirt word for word. *It's not how you play the game; it's how you look when you play the game.*

"Too bad about sectionals," I say. "And I guess you'll need a new shirt."

"What?" she spits.

"Turns out it's really *all* about how you play the game."

Bianca drops her water bottle and stares at me.

"Hey!" Ellen snaps. "Pick that up. *Now.*"

I think Bianca is in shock. She picks it up.

Mrs. Loring is still on the top step, holding my leaf project. I reach up, flip the switch Zig installed, and walk away to meet him while the leaves spin and twirl behind me.

CHAPTER 26

Mom and Nonna are having tea at the kitchen table when we get back. Tea and cookies, and judging by the crumbs on her sweater, Mom's been holding her own in the cookie department. She's writing while she eats.

"Then sort of mix the butter with a fork until it's nice and creamy." Nonna makes whisking motions with her right hand.

"Mix butter until creamy," Mom mumbles, writing.

"With a fork."

"I just wrote mix until creamy."

"Well, you'll need to add 'with a fork.' It has to be with a fork."

"Honestly, Mom, I can't see how—"

Mom stops talking and adds "with a fork." It's amazing how the right look from your mother shuts you up instantly, even when you're forty-three years old.

Mom looks up at me. "Well?"

I smile big-time. "I'm going to sectionals."

"That's my girl!" Nonna says.

"I missed practice, so I need to go for a run after Zig goes home. He helped me all afternoon." I look over at him. "And completely saved me."

"Well, no . . ." Zig looks down at the cookie plate. "I just provided some electrical consulting. Can I have one of these?" He pulls up a chair as the doorbell rings.

"I got it!" Dad yells from the living room.

"Help yourself. I'm writing down Nonna's recipes." Mom reaches for another index card.

"So I don't forget them," Nonna adds.

"You'd never forget the recipe for the wedding cookies!" I say. And then I remember. She probably will. And my eyes well up again.

"Bella faccia." Nonna lifts a wrinkled hand to my chin and tips it up. "Beautiful face," she calls me. Even with my red nose and puffy, watery eyes.

She moves her hand up to my cheek and brushes away my tears. "I may not always be here, *bella,* but here I am now. And here you are." She turns to Mom, who is scribbling recipes like her life depends on it. "And here's my Angela. We're all here, right now, and right now is the best we can do."

There's a knock at the kitchen door.

It's Ruby, holding her bike helmet and a big blue binder. She steps inside. "I wanted to show you something." She slides the binder onto the table and flips open the cover. Inside is the picture of her with her grandmother at fifth-grade graduation. The picture Dad used to dress her for the funeral. The picture Ruby loved so much.

I turn the pages carefully and watch Mrs. Kinsella's life flip by, in color photographs and black and white, in letters and movie tickets and pressed flowers. It's a scrapbook. No, a memory book. And it's the most beautiful thing I've ever seen.

Ruby's smiling. "I finished it this afternoon, now that the leaf collection's out of the way. I wanted to show you because you helped me say good-bye." She turns a page in the binder, to a picture of her grandmother standing by the shore of a lake in one of those bathing suits with the skirts. It's hot pink. She's laughing, like whoever is taking the picture just said something hilarious. Ruby taps the picture. "This is what I want to remember."

Ian zips into the room, sliding on his socks on the wood floor like a baseball player trying to get to second base. He's safe. And he's holding something behind his back. When we start to look at Ruby's memory book, he whips out Dad's camera—Dad's expensive camera—and snaps a picture. He's somehow managed to find a setting that causes it to make loud shutter noises when he takes a photo, even though it's digital.

Ka-chick. Ruby leaning on the table.

Ka-chick. Mom reaching for another cookie.

Ka-chick. A close-up of Ruby's red high-tops.

Ka-chick. Nonna sipping her tea.

Ka-chick. Zig and I looking at the memory book, standing so close our shoulders are touching. *Ka-chick! Ka-chick! Ka-chick!*

"Ian Thomas Zales!" The full-name treatment from Mom. Ian better run. "What on earth possessed you to take your father's digital camera and—"

"Wait!" I grab Ian's arm just as he's about to take off and disappear into a paparazzi getaway car. "Let me see that camera a minute."

I hit the review button and start thumbing through the

digital images stored inside. Ian must have heisted this camera off Dad's desk days ago. There are more than a hundred pictures, some of them pretty good ones.

There's a whole bunch of Nonna baking. There are close-ups of her hands measuring flour. Her oven mitt, easing a tray of cookies onto the rack to cool. Her face, as she leans down to breathe in the cookies cooling on the paper bag.

There are medium shots where you see all of Nonna in her flowered dress and knee-high nylons sagging around her ankles.

And there are long shots—Nonna in her kitchen, where she's the queen of food and love.

Ian is a genius.

"You've got to let him keep using this." I pass the camera over to Mom before she can object, and I watch her eyes water as she scans through the pictures of Nonna. "We can make a memory book for Nonna—so she'll have it later, when she can't remember things by herself." I'm getting excited now. "We can have pictures of everyone with their names, and family stories . . ."

"And Nonna-isms," Zig says. "All her quotes and words of wisdom and . . . uh . . . predictions."

"And recipes," Mom adds.

"You should have older pictures, too." Ruby shows us one of her grandmother as a little girl.

"And pressed flowers," I add.

"No. Leaves." Nonna pats me on the hand. "I like leaves better."

"I have a bunch of old pictures next to the bookshelf." Mom heads into the living room.

"I've got that binder upstairs from my leaf collection—I mean *Mom's* leaf collection."

"I can help with the cutting and arranging pages," Ruby offers. The pages in her grandmother's book are bright and just feel good, like a story with a happy ending.

Deep inside, I know this story won't have one, but right now, I just want to feel better for a little while. And someday, when Nonna can't remember my name anymore—maybe one year from now, maybe five—I want to remember her voice, and her stories, and her cookies, and days like today.

Maybe it will help.

I run upstairs to get the one red maple leaf I have left from my project, but I stop halfway down.

Ruby's flipping through her grandmother's memory book, showing Nonna pictures. They're smiling. Mom and Zig are flipping through old pictures. They're laughing at the one of me in the tub when I was three. Dad is in the kitchen, sneaking cookies while Mom is busy. And Ian just caught him on camera. With his new status as family memory keeper, Ian is on a mission.

Ka-chick. Dad's guilty cookie face.

Ka-chick. Ruby's smile.

Ka-chick. Mom's hand on Nonna's arm.

He's snapping photographs like every second counts, like every moment matters.

And it does.

As we sort through pictures so old their corners are yellow and soft and pictures so new Ian's smile shows missing teeth that still haven't grown back, the sun slips lower into the neighbor's oak tree. I've pretty much given up the idea of a run tonight, even though I was itching to go.

I feel like I should stay to trim the corners and press leaves and be the glue-stick person so Ian doesn't get goop all over the table.

But Nonna catches me looking out the window.

"Go," she says. She nods at the orange glow painting the curtains. "You're going to miss the prettiest light of the day if you don't get moving."

"And you have sectionals to get ready for now," Zig says. "I'll hang out here until you get back."

"No, I'll stay. I don't want to miss everybody."

"I'll be here." Zig grins. "At least as long as the cookies hold out."

"I'll be here, too," Nonna says, and gives me a shove out of my chair. "Go. It's good for you."

Somehow, Nonna always knows.

"Tie your shoes," Mom says.

"I was going to."

"I know." She watches me tie them. "Sometimes I like to tell you anyway, okay?"

"Okay." I make double knots, bound down the steps, and open the door. A bunch of oak leaves scuttle in onto the welcome mat, as if they'd rung the doorbell and waited forever for somebody to show up. I step out and pull the door shut behind me before more blow in. I push against it to stretch my calves and start at a jog down Washington Street. It's empty except for maple leaves from our front yard scratching across the street to crowd up against Mrs. Warren's fence.

Mr. Webster's catalpa tree is mostly bare. Its dry,

elephant-ear leaves are flying everywhere. I love it when I step right on one and my foot lands with a big crunch instead of just a little thud, so I try to step on as many as I can without breaking my stride, but it's hard and I'm weaving all over the place, and finally I see Mr. Webster looking out his office window, laughing, so I stop and run straight again. Focus.

The sun's still out, but it's sinking closer to a bank of dark clouds over the lake—the TV weather guy with the huge smile said there's a storm coming overnight. Rain, maybe sleet. Even through the sunshine, great gusts of wind are picking up by the minute, whipping leaves off their branches, whirling them into a last dance before the snow.

I love it when they fall on me. Especially the little ones. It's like running through confetti.

The honey locust in Mr. Nelson and Mr. Collins's yard showers down tiny leaves that look like teardrops. I hold out my hand and try to catch them while I run through.

"Still working on that leaf project, Gianna?" Mr. Collins is trimming a bright red shrub in their garden. Mr. Nelson holds open the trash bag for him.

"No! I finally finished this afternoon."

"Did you include our Kentucky coffee tree?" Mr. Nelson asks.

"Honey locust." Mr. Collins tosses another branch into the trash bag.

"It is no such thing," Mr. Nelson says, "and I certainly hope she didn't label it as one in her project. She'll flunk."

"*You'd* flunk. It's a honey locust." Mr. Collins tosses another branch, but he misses the bag because Mr. Nelson has pulled it away and closed it.

"I know a Kentucky coffee tree when I see one, James."

"Actually, he's right," I say. "Zig and I checked our leaf guide. It's a honey locust." Mr. Nelson drops his yard bag like I just slapped him. "Sorry. Kentucky coffee trees are bigger and usually have seed pods, too."

"Told you." Mr. Collins shakes his branch.

"Hmph." Mr. Nelson opens the yard bag again, and they get back to work.

"Thanks for the leaves anyway." I pick up my pace and pass Mr. Randolph's house. His miserable black walnut tree looks even more poisonous than usual. I hope they're happy together.

By the time I hit Drummond Street, I don't even feel the bite of the wind anymore. Just the pounding of my feet and my heart and the leaves dancing around me. I reach out to see how many I can catch as they fly past.

Maple. Catalpa. Birch. Oak.

I turn the corner for home as the sun drops into the clouds. Our five pumpkins wait for me on the porch, and Zig's bike in the yard makes me smile.

I put on a last burst of speed, but with my hands full of leaves, it's hard to keep my stride, and the wind's blowing harder. It wants its leaves back.

I slow down and hold them in front of me like a bouquet.

Maple. Catalpa. Birch. Oak.

Scarlet-orange. Dark green-gold. Ripe banana yellow. And rich, warm brown.

I hold them to my face, breathe in, and let them go.

They dance off into the end of October.

And I run.

ACKNOWLEDGMENTS

I offer bouquets of autumn leaves and many, many thanks to everyone who helped bring this book into the world:

Writer friends Julie Berry, Linda Urban, Linda Salzman, Bonnie Shimko, Loree Griffin-Burns, Ammi-Joan Paquette Tanya Lee Stone, and the rest of the Kindling Words crew, Judith Mammay, Candice Hayden, Gail Lenhard, Marjorie Light, and Stephanie Gorin. Whether you critiqued this book in its early stages, organized the retreat where it was revised, or just listened, it wouldn't be as bright without you.

Early readers Amy DeMane, Molly Schneider-Ferrari, and Eunice Choe, who helped me fix the spots where the kids weren't talking like real kids.

Dick and Lorraine Walker of Walker Funeral Home, who taught me about life and death in a funeral home family.

Kevin Larkin, my consultant on all things cross-country.

My friends on Verla Kay's Blue Boards, who chimed in with thoughts on everything from Italian grandmothers to not giving up.

Science teacher Barbara Napper, who started the leaf collection that started it all and taught me much about leaves and life along the way.

The SMS English Department—Andrew Ducharme, Marjorie Light, Karen Rock, Nancy Strack, Michelle Walpole, and librarian Russell Puschak, who connect kids with books every day.

My fantastic agent, Jennifer Laughran of Andrea Brown Literary, whose guidance made this book stronger and found it a perfect home, and whose tenacity and love of books never cease to amaze me.

The fantastic folks at Walker whose hard work shines in these pages: copyeditor Sandy Smith, designer Nicole Gastonguay, and everyone else.

My delightful editor, Mary Kate Castellani, whose brilliant ideas and enthusiasm helped bring Gianna's story to life.

The Schirmers, Rupperts, Messners, and Alois—family members who have joined me on this journey, encouraged me along the way, and put up with my daydreaming and bouncing of ideas. I'd imagine it's been sort of like living with Ian's riddles.

Jake and Ella, my companions in leaf catching, birch swinging, and memory making. Thanks for being terrific kids and letting me borrow little bits of your lives for my stories.

And Tom, my husband and best friend, who is tough to pin down but might be a cross between a white oak and a sugar maple, bright and full of energy and steady, all at once.

Nonna's Funeral Cookies

Ingredients

1 ½ cups butter

> *Before you ask, the answer is no. You may not substitute some fat-free butter replacement if you want the cookies to come out like mine.*

¾ cup confectioners' sugar
½ tsp salt
1 ½ cups finely ground almonds

> *You have to grind them the old-fashioned way, with a mortar and pestle, if you want the cookies to turn out right. The ground almonds should look almost like flour. If you use one of those newfangled food processors, you're going to end up with big, sharp slivers of almond in the middle of your cookies, and they won't melt in your mouth like they're supposed to. If you're in a super hurry or you don't have a mortar and pestle, go ahead and use a food processor, but don't say I didn't warn you.*

5 tsp vanilla extract

> *For goodness' sake, make sure it's the real stuff and not imitation vanilla extract.*

3 cups flour
Another ½ cup confectioners' sugar (set this aside for rolling)

Directions

1. Wash your hands.

2. Preheat your oven to 325°. Get a cookie sheet ready. Don't grease it. Just leave it alone for now.

3. Mix butter with a fork until it's soft, and nice and creamy. Gradually add confectioners' sugar and salt, stirring the whole time. Try to keep it from getting stuck on the sides of the bowl. Then add the ground almonds, vanilla extract, and flour.

4. Rub a little butter on your hands so they're greasy. This will keep the dough from sticking to them when you handle it. Roll the dough into little balls (use about a teaspoon for each cookie) and place them on the ungreased cookie sheet.

5. Bake the cookies for 15–20 minutes. Take them out before they get brown! Let them cool for about five minutes, and then, while they're still warm, roll them in the remaining confectioners' sugar. Enjoy!

XOXO
~Nonna

What Kind of Tree Are You?

If you were a tree, what kind would you be?
Take this quiz to find out!

1. **When you have a big project due at school, you're most likely to:**

    a. Work on it a little bit every day until it's done. You'll probably finish before the deadline.

    b. Spend about half of your time working on your own project and the other half helping friends.

    c. Tell your parents you're working on your project but actually hang out in your room listening to music. You'll meet your deadline but might need to copy from a friend at the last minute.

    d. Put off working on the project but finish it in a big, creative flurry at the end. It won't be perfect, but it'll be interesting!

    e. Make sure the project looks good first. You'll probably win an award for the neatest project and shiniest binder.

    f. Work hard with whatever materials you have to do the best project possible. You'll finish on time, no matter what obstacles stand in your way.

2. **When you come home from school, you find that your brother or sister has been rummaging around your bedroom. You're likely to handle the situation by:**

a. Having a calm discussion about your property and your right to privacy.

b. Helping to find what he or she was looking for and offering to share it anytime.

c. Telling your parents, then sneaking into your brother's or sister's bedroom and throwing things around to make a mess.

d. Devising a creative way to booby-trap your room—maybe a string tied to the doorknob that causes a bucket of feathers to fall on anyone who enters without your permission!

e. Putting everything back in place, exactly where it was. You can't stand to have your room a mess.

f. Making it clear to your sibling that you expect your privacy to be respected, and also talking with your parents.

3. **It's Halloween. You're mostly likely to spend the night:**

a. Dressing up in a simple costume to answer the door for trick-or-treaters and then going out to collect candy yourself.

b. Volunteering at a party for underprivileged kids.

c. Roaming the neighborhood, decorating cars in toilet paper.

d. Creating an elaborate haunted house with moving ghosts, carved pumpkins, paper spiders, and spooky sound effects for the trick-or-treaters at your house to enjoy.

e. Getting decked out in a perfect—absolutely perfect—

costume for a party with your friends. You'll bring elaborately decorated jack-o'-lantern cupcakes.

f. Trick-or-treating at every single house in the neighborhood. You'll be out every possible minute so you don't miss out on a single candy bar.

4. **Your gym teacher says you have to run a mile in less than ten minutes in class next week. You prepare by:**

a. Running a little every day to get in shape and work your way up to a mile.

b. Checking in with your friends to encourage them and see if they need any help training.

c. Figuring out a shortcut so you can have the best time without even breaking a sweat.

d. Loading up your iPod with the songs that you think will help you run the fastest.

e. Going shopping for a new running outfit. As long as you look good, it doesn't matter if you make it in ten minutes or not.

f. Running a mile before school every morning and timing yourself until you can do it in eight minutes flat. That way, you won't be taking any chances.

5. **You find out that one of your friends is having a big birthday bash and hasn't invited you. You would probably:**

a. Just wait and see what happens. Maybe he or she just forgot, and if not, you'll find something else to do.

b. Burst into tears. But then you buy him or her a gift anyway.

c. Start a rumor about that friend so no one else will want to go to the birthday party either.

d. Lavish your friend with homemade birthday cards as a reminder to invite you.

e. Wear your coolest outfit to school the next day so your friend will be sure to notice and remember to send your invitation.

f. Take a deep breath and ask your friend if he or she is upset with you. Being honest is scary sometimes, but confronting the problem is usually the best approach.

6. **For *your* birthday, your plans would most likely include:**

a. Just the usual . . . a family party with cake and a few presents.

b. Requesting that people who come to your party donate to your favorite charity instead of purchasing gifts.

c. Having a fabulous party and talking it up big-time at school, making sure that everyone knows who's invited and who isn't.

d. Planning your own party decorations, right down to the homemade piñata.

e. Begging your parents to hire a party planner and caterer so everything is perfect on your big day.

f. A busy day of activity—maybe a hike up a mountain or extra-long bike ride—before the cake and ice cream.

7. **You find out that a girl you know is spreading rumors about you at school. You handle the situation by:**

a. Ignoring her and waiting for it to blow over.

b. Offering to help her with her homework in study hall. Maybe she's feeling frustrated about her classes and that's why she's being mean.

c. "Accidentally" pouring chocolate milk all over her homework folder during lunch.

d. Laughing at it. In fact, you put together your own tabloid newspaper for your friends, with her gossip included as silly headlines on the front page.

e. Talking to people to make sure they know those rumors aren't true.

f. Confronting the girl, asking her why she's targeting you, and telling her to knock it off.

How many times did you answer with each letter?

a _____
b _____
c _____
d _____
e _____
f _____

The letter with the highest score will match you up with the perfect tree.

a) You're a red oak. You have a sure, steady personality and don't like to draw attention to yourself. You're easygoing but strong. Don't be afraid to try new things once in a while; that's how you'll grow.

Red oak trees don't have showy leaves in autumn, but they're among the last trees to lose their leaves. Red oaks are tolerant of many different kinds of soil—not particularly high-maintenance trees. The wood of the red oak is strong and useful and often used in furniture.

b) You're a weeping willow. You're sensitive and kind, and you love helping other people, even when that means putting their needs ahead of your own. Make sure you take care of yourself too!

Weeping willow trees have slender branches and long, feathery leaves that some butterfly larvae use as food. The leaves and bark of the willow have long been used as medicine, since they contain a substance called salicylic acid, a very early version of aspirin.

c) You're a black walnut. You're popular and attractive, but you might have more to learn about kindness and trust. When you're dealing with your peers, try to think about how you'd like to be treated.

Black walnuts are pretty trees that require a good amount of light. Parts of the black walnut tree, including the roots, give off a poisonous substance called "juglone" that can inhibit or kill other plants growing nearby, but its fruit (the nuts) ripen in the fall and can be used for food.

d) You're a sugar maple. You're sweet, energetic, fluttery, and creative, even if you do seem a little scattered sometimes. Just make sure you can focus all that positive energy when you need to get something accomplished!

Sugar maples are deciduous trees whose leaves turn bright red, orange, and yellow in the fall, so you might see four or five different colors on a tree at once. They are an important part of the New England, New York, and Canadian economies thanks to their sap, which is boiled down into sweet maple syrup in the spring.

e) You're a European mountain ash. You're one of those people who always look fantastic, even when you've just woken up. But that's no accident—you take great pride in your appearance and know it's a reflection of who you are. Just remember what's inside matters even more.

The European mountain ash is an ornamental tree known for its clusters of white flowers in spring and its showy display of orange red berry clusters in early autumn. It is not tolerant of heat or drought and requires pruning to stay in good condition.

f) You're an American beech. You are one tough cookie, and when you set your mind on something, look out! Your determination and courage are impressive, but don't forget that nobody is tough all the time. Don't be afraid to give yourself a break.

The American beech tree is a shade-tolerant species with leathery leaves. If you walk in the woods in the winter, you'll often see brown beech leaves still clinging to their branches long after the other leaves have fallen. The wood of the American beech is tough, strong, and heavy and was so difficult to cut that loggers often left it alone in the days before chain saws.

Reading Group Guide for
The Brilliant Fall of Gianna Z.

1. A person's room can say a lot about his or her personality. Do you think Gianna's bedroom reflects her personality? What do the things in your bedroom say about you?

2. Frustrated with a test, Gianna says, "I'm not a one-bubble kind of girl" (p. 45). Do you think Gianna is referring only to tests? Are you a "one-bubble" kind of person? What about you makes you "one-bubble" or not?

3. Why do you think Gianna is so upset when she hears about Ruby's grandmother? Gianna worries about what she'll say to Ruby at the funeral home. What advice would you give her? Have you ever needed to comfort a friend who has lost someone they love? What kinds of things did you say or do to try to comfort them?

4. In English class, Gianna is introduced to the poem "Birches," by Robert Frost. Why do you think this poem speaks to Gianna? Do you like "Birches"? What does the poem say to you?

5. Dealing with changes in life can be difficult—especially when it is a loved one who changes. Gianna and her mother have different responses to the changes in Nonna. Why do

you think they react differently to the same events? If you were in Gianna's place, how do you think you would react? Have you ever faced a similar situation in your own life? How did you deal with the changes you faced?

6. How would you describe Gianna's relationship with Zig in the beginning of the book? Does it seem to be changing? If so, how? Gianna seems to appreciate Zig more as her family situation gets more difficult. Do you think he's a good friend? Why or why not?

7. When Gianna is up in the tree, she watches and listens to her mother and grandmother and says, ". . . it's a little easier to imagine a Mom other than the list-making, tofu-eating, three-ring-binder-organizing Mom of right now" (p. 103). Why do you think she's suddenly able to see her mom in a different way? How do you see your own mother? Has the way you think of your mom changed?

8. How would you have reacted if you found what Gianna found when she returned to the locker room? Why do you think she chose not to tell her coach what happened? Would you have made the same choice?

9. Everything possible seems to be going wrong with Gianna's leaf project. Do you think any of the problems are her fault? What do you think of the way Gianna's mother solved the leaf-collection problem? Should Gianna turn in

the project? Why do you think Gianna feels worse when she sees the other students' leaf projects? Do you think the new leaf collection is a better reflection of Gianna's personality? Why or why not?

10. What role do you think Ian plays in the Zales family? Does anyone in your family remind you of Ian?

11. What do you think of Gianna's mother's plans to keep Nonna safe? What other suggestions might you make to the family?

12. Would you consider the ending of this book a happy one? Why or why not?

Kate Messner is a middle-school teacher who has helped with hundreds of leaf collection projects over the years. She's especially fond of catalpa trees and sugar maples. Kate lives on Lake Champlain with her husband and two kids and loves spending time in the woods.

www.katemessner.com

The ice isn't the coldest thing
at the Silver Blades figure
skating program...

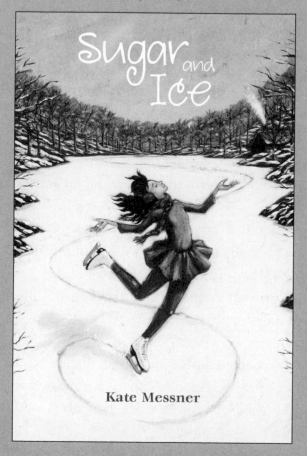

Will Claire be able to make the final cut, or will she be
frozen in place by some of the meanest girls on ice?

Read on for a sneak peek of Kate Messner's next novel.

"And I believe you are the last skater. Let us see what you can do on a real rink." He opened the door of the penalty box, and Claire took a step toward the ice on wobbly knees.

"I . . . didn't bring music," she said.

He stared at her. Did this man not understand what that kind of look did to a girl's insides? Or did he understand perfectly?

"I know I was supposed to bring a CD, but I was wondering . . . Well, I've skated to 'Autumn,' the song that Meghan had? I was thinking . . . I wondered if . . ."

Andrei Groshev snapped his fingers at the penalty box. "Meghan. Your music is with Bella yet, yes?"

Meghan nodded. "Why?"

"Go tell her that Claire will skate to the same song today."

Meghan's eyes widened. "Is that your music for competitions? I still use it sometimes even though I'm working on a new routine."

"Oh, no, I don't do competitions. I mean, I haven't much," Claire said. "It was just my music for the Maple Show."

Alexis stepped forward and snorted out a laugh. "The *Maple Show*?" She turned to Meghan. "I don't think you need to worry. Let's go tell Bella to cue up the music for Mrs.

Butterworth here." She clattered up the stairs with Meghan behind her.

Claire's throat went dry. She looked at Groshev, waiting for him to say something. But he either didn't hear or didn't care. He just looked down at Claire. "Should you not be on the ice?"

She skated out and struck her opening pose, her heart pounding, until Vivaldi's first notes filled the rink for the second time.

Claire started slowly. What if she fell in front of Groshev her first day here? Maybe they'd take back her scholarship. Could they do that already? There was no way she could skate like Alexis.

Stop, she thought. *Stop. Just skate.* And she did, into the second turn—the one with the tough footwork pattern. And she did it.

Just skate. As the song picked up its pace, Claire's heart finally slowed down so she could hear the music over its pounding. She loved this song, the way the notes seemed to hold the memory of every step of the routine and give them all back to her just in time. She felt her movements grow quicker, lighter, like Tasanee's. Like a butterfly. She turned away from the penalty box and smiled.

She pushed harder than usual, gearing up for the big jump. Groshev would expect her to land it; he'd already seen it. But she forced that thought from her mind, forced it from her muscles, and instead let the music fill her like helium in a balloon.

She jumped, higher than she had at the Maple Show, even, she could tell. She turned above the ice and landed firmly, arms out, leg stretched behind her, and a smile that met Andrei Groshev straight on. She twirled away for the final sequence. But not before she saw him smiling back. And this time, she was sure.

∞

It was 4:50, but before they went back to the locker room, Andrei Groshev called them to stand around the circle at center ice. He stood in the middle and rotated slowly, meeting all of their eyes as he spoke.

"You have put in a full day. That is good, for a start. But make no mistake: you have a long, long way to go if you are even to think about competing nationally. You will not make it if you are not giving everything that you have." Claire saw his eyes rest on Stevie for a second.

"Skating here is not a right. It is not something that you are entitled to." He paused. "It is a privilege that some of you may not have much longer if I am not seeing you grow. If I am not seeing the commitment. The passion." Across the circle from Claire, Meghan twisted her braid and looked at the floor.

"But some of you," Groshev pivoted until he was facing Claire, and she felt everyone's eyes on her. "Some of you have impressed me today." She should have felt proud; she should have been absolutely bursting. He liked her! He liked her skating! But her knees shook.

Groshev held up a stack of papers. "Take a schedule, and then you are dismissed." Claire's hand shook as she reached for the paper.

Groshev held on to it for a moment and looked down at her. "Very nice work today." Claire squeaked out a "thank you" and skated toward the boards but sensed someone too close behind her. When she turned, she saw what she had already felt—Alexis's eyes burning into her, cold as ice.

Did you like watching leaves fall with Gianna Z.?

Then you'll love Allie Jo's magical adventures in